The Stone of Mercy

BOOK ONE OF THE CENTAUR CHRONICLES

THE CENTAUR CHRONICLES

BOOK 1

THE STONE OF MERCY

M.J. Evans

M.J. Evans/Dancing Horse Press

7013 S. Telluride St.

Foxfield, CO 80017

www.dancinghorsepress.com

Book Layout ©2015 BookDesignTemplates.com

Ordering Information:

Quantity sales. Special discounts are available on quantity purchases by corporations, associations, and others. For details, contact the "Special Sales Department" at the address above.

The Stone of Mercy/ M.J. Evans. —1st ed.

ISBN 978-0-9966617-4-4

DANCING HORSE PRESS

The Stone of Mercy is dedicated to all the fantasy-lovers who are willing to serve where and when they are called.

And to my Grandchildren that I love around the world and back!

Contents

"Stand therefore,

having your loins girt

about with truth, and having on the

breastplate of righteousness."

Eph. 6:16 (KJV)

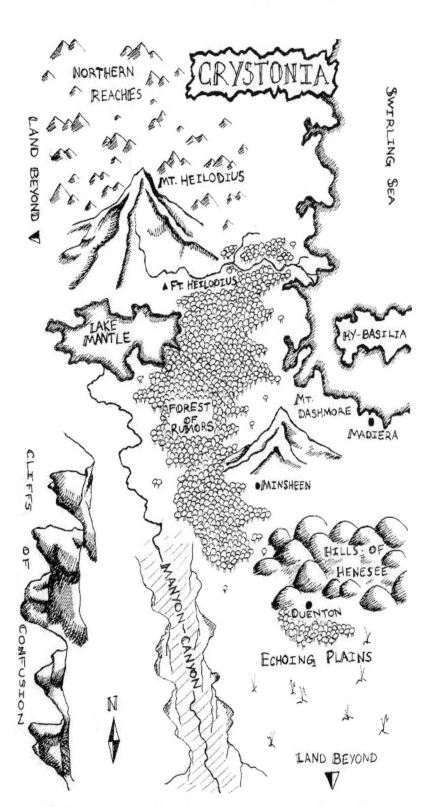

CHAPTER 1

A Visit from the Wizard

THE BLACKSMITH'S FOOT EXPERTLY pumped the bellows as he turned the piece of iron first one way then the other in the bright orange coals. The glow emanating from the little forge provided the only light as the sun began its descent behind the western hogback. Intense heat caused beads of sweat to roll down the narrow patch of skin that separated the smithy's thick black hair from his single bushy eyebrow. The long brow served as a miniature breakwater, sending the sweat to the right and left before releasing it to run down the sides of his round, puffy face in great droplets. None of this mattered to the Duende, who was accustomed to the discomfort imposed upon him by his chosen profession.

The strip of metal was now glowing brightly in the same shade of orange as the coals into which it had been thrust. Tightly clasping the iron with his fire tongs, the smithy pulled it from the forge and quickly turned around toward his anvil.

The shock of seeing the tall, thin, hooded figure looming over him caused him to drop the metal strip, sending it bouncing off his boot and leaving a burn mark on the leather toe. The metal clanged loudly on the ash-covered stone floor. His breath caught in his throat.

"I'm sorry that I startled you." The deep, sinuous voice came from beneath the gray hood that covered the stranger's head and concealed his face.

"I...I...I wasn't exactly expecting anyone," stammered Ashtic, the village's only blacksmith. His heart pounding, he wiped his glistening forehead with the back of his sleeve, painting it with a streak of soot, then rubbed his hands on his scarred leather apron. "May I help you with something?"

"My name is Vidente and it is I who have come to help you and your race." The stranger stood up even taller before continuing. "A queen is soon to be born who will bring peace to the land. She will be one of your kind. She will be a Duende."

"A Duende?" echoed Ashtic in the squeaky voice typical of all the Duende, dubious that a queen could be chosen from his race.

The Duende were shy, quiet creatures, descendants of the fairies that once populated the land. Their features were fine, their ears pointed, remnants of their fairy heritage. They were known and respected as artisans who kept to themselves.

They were also recognized for their intelligence coupled with wisdom, but had never been considered as the source for a monarch due to their small stature and peace-loving ways. Yet, no other race had been able to maintain the throne for longer than a decade, and now the land of Crystonia had been without a ruler for the past century and a half. For the same amount of time, there had been no peace in the land while the larger, stronger races battled for leadership. The Centaurs, Ogres, and Cyclops all wanted to conquer and maintain Mount Heilodius, the designated location of the empire's seat of government.

The Duende had always sided with the Centaurs, hoping that the race of half human-half horse would ascend to the top. The Centaurs were wise and peace-loving creatures as well, with the strength and size to win a battle, if necessary. But now, even that race had splintered into two factions, one still motivated by justice and mercy; the other by power and control.

"Yes. One of your women is already with child. In four months' time, she will be delivered of a daughter, the future queen."

"Does this woman know the child she is carrying is destined to become a queen?" asked Ashtic, still skeptical.

"Not yet. I need to call upon your skills before I visit with her."

"My skills? What skills do I have that could help a queen?" said Ashtic as he lit a lantern overhead. The yellow light did little to reveal the features of this stranger, making them even harder to discern as a dark shadow from the man's cloak cut across his face.

"You are the best smithy in all of Crystonia, or so I am told," said the stranger kindly. "I need you to make a silver breastplate for the future queen."

"A breastplate?" Ashtic was both confused and intrigued. "What would you have it look like?"

The stranger reached into his cloak and withdrew a roll of parchment, then brushed aside the tools scattered haphazardly across a low wooden table that was so old the grain stood up in tiny ridges. Carefully, he unrolled and spread out the parchment, the ends of which fell over the sides of the table.

The stranger's hands were long and narrow, his nails clean but untrimmed, the skin fair and unblemished. Ashtic noted the sizable rings that graced the center fingers on both hands. Each ring was made of silver and had beautiful engravings on the bands. One held a large red stone; the other, an equally large blue stone.

After smoothing out the document, the stranger traced its drawing. Ashtic followed the movement with his eyes. "What is it?" he asked.

"The queen's breastplate." The visitor spoke softly and slowly, articulating each word. "This is what I need you to make to enable the future queen to save all the races of Crystonia. The rightful wearer of this breastplate, when it is complete, will have the power and authority to rule the land in righteousness."

The little smithy chewed on his bottom lip and twisted his untrimmed beard as he examined the drawing. The breastplate was carefully sketched, its dimensions clearly labeled. He marveled at the intricate and curious curving designs that covered the body of the shell. They resembled twisted vines adorned with blossoms. Most unusual were the four round holes on the plate, the largest in the center and three others forming an equilateral triangle around it. The Duende realized this was going to be a difficult task if he was to recreate the design just as it was drawn.

As if the stranger could read his thoughts, the tall, mysterious visitor said, "It is of utmost importance that you follow these directions with diligence. There can be no variation in the slightest." He pointed to each of the circular holes. "These holes will hold the four Stones of Light. Each one endows the wearer with certain necessary powers. Powers that make for a great and noble leader. The one on the lower left is for the Stone of Mercy, the one on the right, the Stone of Courage."

He moved his finger and touched the circle at the top. "This one is for the Stone of Integrity." Moving his long finger to the center and largest circle, he said, "And this will hold the Stone of Wisdom."

Ashtic shook his head slowly as he studied the plans. "I can create the silver breastplate. But where will I get the stones?"

The stranger chuckled kindly. "Oh, my friend, do not worry about the stones. That will not be your job. That will be the quest of your future queen." Then the visitor paused. "Yes, it will be her quest, if she can do it." He paused again before adding, "I don't want to think about what would happen if she was to fail."

The smithy looked up into the face of the stranger. Only his eyes were visible, but they were eyes filled with an intensity he had never seen before. Ashtic was overwhelmed by the realization that he was being asked to play a small part in a very important mission.

The blacksmith looked down at the parchment again. As he did so, his visitor slid the diagram off the table and rolled it up. In the blink of an eye, the stranger was gone. Ashtic ran to the door of his shop and looked up and down the village street. The road was muddy from the recent rains, the smell of the rain and wet earth still heavy in the air. The shops all around him were quiet, and he watched as lanterns were turned on, their yellow glow shining through lead-paned windows as the sun settled in the west.

But there was no sign of a hooded, caped stranger.

CHAPTER 2

Saleen

THE LOVELY YOUNG DUENDE female rubbed her belly. She already loved the new life growing within her, even though its birth was still months away. She sighed with contentment and returned her attention to her weaving. The mother-in-waiting hummed a lullaby as she worked at her loom, sending the shuttle back and forth through the shed formed by the warp yarns and pressing the weft tight with the reed and batten. Of all the Duende, her family was the most accomplished in the art of weaving. Saleen had learned the art from her mother, who had been carefully taught by her grandmother and so forth back through the generations, farther back than anyone could now remember.

She paused to count her rows, calculating when she needed to put in a new color of yarn. Suddenly aware that she was not alone, she jerked her head up and looked through the loom. Standing just a few feet away, but well inside the room, was a tall, thin figure. Saleen could not tell if the creature was a man or a woman, nor what race it was. Her beautiful face with its fine features turned ashen. Her heart started pounding. Her breathing became shallow, and she could feel beads of sweat pop out on her forehead.

"May I...I...help you?" the young Duende stammered.

"I have come with important news," the creature said without moving any closer.

Saleen squinted her eyes against the sun that was coming through the window and lighting the dancing specks of dust behind the stranger. She tried to get a clearer picture of what her visitor looked like, but without success. "Please, sir, tell me who you are."

"I am called Vidente. I have been sent from afar with an important message for you," said the visitor, his voice calm and soothing.

Saleen sensed no threat and felt herself relax. "What might this important message be?" she asked.

"The child you carry in your womb has a responsibility to fulfill. It is she who has been chosen to become the queen of Crystonia. But she must first fulfill many difficult and dangerous assignments in order to become qualified to rule."

Saleen gasped. She could not believe what she was hearing. One part of her wanted to sing for joy that her child was to become a queen. But the words "difficult" and "dangerous" seemed to overshadow the good news. Fear enveloped her. Fear for her unborn child. She wrapped her arms around her swollen belly in an effort to protect her child. *My baby is a girl. My baby is a queen,* she thought to herself. *But my child will be in danger.*

She lifted her eyes and looked toward the bearer of such great and terrible news. "Why my baby? Why her?"

"She has been chosen. I do not know why. I am merely the messenger. There is much I need to tell you. I will leave you for now. But I will be back before she is born to tell you more." The tall figure moved silently backward and then was gone.

Saleen dropped her shuttle, which rattled on the stone floor. She didn't notice. The stunned young mother continued to stare into the empty space where the stranger, who called himself Vidente, had just stood. She was alone again. Alone with her thoughts and her unborn child.

The child, *her* child, was to become a queen. She pondered this information in her heart. Yet, all the while, the words "difficult" and "dangerous" filtered through her mind. Could she really allow her child to face anything so ominous? From the moment she'd known she was pregnant, Saleen had only dreamed of an ordinary life for this child growing within her...she wanted her to find the wonder and marvel of an ordinary life. *No, this cannot be,* she told herself. *There must be some mistake.*

CHAPTER 3

The Silver Breastplate

IT HAD BEEN NEARLY two months since the stranger's visit to the village of Duenton, the home of the tiny and industrious Duende. On the Wizard's previous visit, only two villagers had seen him: Ashtic, the blacksmith, and the pregnant weaver named Saleen. Both had much in common, however. Neither was a town leader. No, they were just two of the many common folk that populated the village. Both, however, were respected for their character and for the quality of the work they produced. And while both held the secret of the stranger's visit in their hearts, they also doubted their own memories. Neither knew that the other had been visited as well.

Late one afternoon, as the winter sun cast its final light over the town square and shadows filled the blacksmith shop, Ashtic turned off his forge and began the daily and tedious task of cleaning up his workspace. He was sweeping the ashes out from under the legs of his heavy wooden worktable when his broom brushed the toe of a pointed boot. The surprise caused by seeing the boots on the far side of his table caused him to jerk upward and hit his head on the edge of the table. He let out a yelp and started rubbing his head as he stood erect. As his eyes moved up the gray cloak until they reached the hooded head, he lowered his hand. "It is you. So I didn't imagine your visit after all."

The stranger chuckled softly. "No, my dear Ashtic, you did not imagine my visit. It was real."

The visitor pulled a scroll out of his cloak and spread it out on the table. Ashtic recognized it at once as the same diagram of a breastplate that he had seen before. He looked up into the shadows that covered the visitor's face. "Is it time to begin?"

"It is."

"Has the child been born?"

"Not yet. She will arrive in two months' time. I need to have the breastplate complete before the babe arrives."

"May I keep the diagram this time?" asked Ashtic, fearing that he might appear to be too presumptuous.

"You may keep it until I come for the queen's breastplate. You must keep this a secret from all others, however. It is imperative that word not get out that the queen's breastplate is being created. Your life, the life of the future queen, and the safety of the residents of this village would be at risk. There are those who would attempt to stop the breastplate from being created. They know its power and the power of the one who wears it. Can you do that? Can you keep it a secret and keep the breastplate and the future queen safe?"

Ashtic swallowed. He could feel his hands getting sweaty. He took a deep breath to calm his pounding heart before answering. "I will try, your honor."

"You cannot merely try. If you take on this task, you must perform it perfectly. You must create the breastplate exactly as the plans specify, and you must keep it hidden from all others."

A flood of confidence suddenly filled the little Duende. "I shall do as you say. It will be perfect. It will be hidden from all."

"Excellent. I will be delivering the silver on the morrow."

"Oh, but I have silver."

"Not like this silver. This is the silver from the Northern Reaches. It is the purest silver ever created. And it is the silver we must use to create the breastplate for the queen."

True to his word, the stranger appeared at Ashtic's shop just as the sun was setting the next day. Over his shoulder he carried a bag that he dropped with a loud thud on the worktable. Ashtic opened the bag and pulled out large chunks of silver. His eyes opened wide in amazement as he examined the pieces of metal. A true lover of all metals, Ashtic was well aware that this was beyond comparison in its purity and beauty. He looked up at the hooded stranger. "It will be an honor to work with this silver. When would you like to return to pick up the completed breastplate?"

"I will be back in six weeks' time." As suddenly as he appeared, the visitor disappeared, leaving Ashtic alone to caress the silver and begin planning the fulfillment of his assignment.

CHAPTER 4

Instructions

ONCE THE SUN BEGAN to go down, Saleen had a difficult time weaving. The fading light made it challenging to distinguish the subtle colors in her pattern. She pressed her hands to her aching lower back and stood, turning away from her loom. The baby was active in her womb and she loved feeling the constant companionship of this little child...a female, the stranger had told her...a queen. Perhaps that was all a dream, she told herself for the hundredth time.

The Duende turned her attention to fixing the evening meal. Her husband would be home soon and she had not yet started anything for supper. She began chopping some vegetables to mix into the rice that was left over from the previous night.

"Saleen."

The little Duende woman jumped in surprise and turned, knife still in hand. Towering over her was the gray robed creature that had visited a few months before.

She dropped her knife, which clattered onto the floor. She didn't know what to say so she stood silently, waiting for him to speak first.

"I have come to give you important instructions."

"Yes, sir," she whispered.

The stranger produced a parcel wrapped in burlap and tied with twine. He set it on the small kitchen table, the wooden table her husband had made for her. The visitor's long delicate fingers untied the twine and parted the burlap covering.

Saleen gasped. There on the table, sparkling with a light of its own, was the most beautiful silver object she had ever seen. "What is it?" she said with awe.

"This is the breastplate of the queen of Crystonia. It gives the wearer the power to rule the land in righteousness."

"It is so beautiful."

"Yes. It is indeed."

Saleen looked up toward the stranger's face. His face was still shaded by his hood, but she could see a sparkle of light coming from his eyes. One hand went to her stomach as she felt her child leap within her womb. "It has been made for her?"

The stranger nodded.

"Are you going to give it to her?"

"No. I will leave it with you. You are to keep it safe until she reaches her sixteenth birthday. At that time, you are to give it to her and her journey will begin."

"What do you mean by 'journey'?" asked Saleen, feeling a sharp stab of fear pierce her heart.

The visitor extended his long arm, revealing his slender fingers once again. Saleen noticed the large blue and red stones set into the rings that adorned both of his center fingers. With one of those fingers, he touched four holes in the breastplate, one at a time. "Each of these will hold a stone of light. When complete, the breastplate will give her both power and protection—the power and protection she will need to rule the land."

Saleen tensed as she felt the first strong contraction flow through her body.

CHAPTER 5

Carling

SALEEN SCURRIED AROUND HER house, preparing a special meal for her daughter's birthday. As she worked, her thoughts reviewed the sixteen years since the birth of her child. *Where has the time gone? How can it have been sixteen years since Carling's birth?* she asked herself.

The lovely dress she'd made for Carling was draped over a chair in the corner. She stopped to admire her handiwork, which included fabric she'd woven herself and stitches that had been carefully placed by her own fingers. She glanced out the front window of their little cottage. The spring flowers, bulbs mostly, painted the countryside with bright colors. They seemed to appear each spring just to honor Carling's birth.

She smiled as she thought of her precious daughter. What joy she had brought to their home. Indeed, everyone in the village loved Carling. Her long auburn hair hung in curls down to her shoulders. Rosy cheeks and red lips colored her face. But most memorable were her violet eyes. They were eyes like no others.

Saleen stopped her reminiscing, turned back to the stove, and bent down to remove a cake from the oven. As she turned, her foot caught on the little rug that covered the wooden floorboards in the center of the kitchen. Hooked on her shoe, the rug slid to one side, uncovering a door that had been built into the floor. Saleen hastily smoothed the rug back over the door, concealing it once again. A pang of guilt flowed through her. For sixteen years, she had kept the burlap package with its precious contents hidden beneath her feet. She knew full well that this was the day she was supposed to give it to her daughter, yet she knew she could not do it. She feared what dangers it would bring and wasn't willing to let her daughter face them, even if doing so might allow her to one day become the queen of Crystonia.

The past sixteen years had seen an escalation in the violence throughout the land as one would-be ruler after another fought for the throne. Saleen had watched in silence, secretly hoping one of them would succeed and the stranger's prediction would prove false. Yet the throne remained empty, and Carling's sixteen birthday had arrived with no ruler for the land.

Not my daughter, Saleen said to herself. *Let someone else do it.*

"Carling, wait for me," Higson shouted as the nimble body of his best friend dashed between the trees and ferns ahead. Carling was taller than he, taller than any of the Duende, in fact. She was slim and graceful and moved elegantly, a fact that Higson surely couldn't help noticing. Seeing her run was like watching a symphony of motion. He was not the only one who had noticed her beauty. He often heard others in the village talk of it. The two, both born on the same day, had been friends their entire lives. Higson was born to a family of hunters, so whenever he could get Carling away from her lessons on the loom, he would school her in the bow and arrow.

Carling loved being in the woods with her friend and, under his tutelage, had become quite adept at using a bow and arrow. Today, her sixteenth birthday, she had wanted nothing more than the chance to spend the day in the forest. Carling knew her mother would not approve of her learning to hunt, so Higson always stored her bow and arrows at his home. On this beautiful spring day, a birthday for both of them, the two friends had met at the edge of the village. There Higson handed over her bow and arrow. Now she was dashing toward the targets they had hung on trees in a beautiful grove, deep within the forest.

As she ran, Carling giggled with delight. "Catch me if you can, slowpoke," she shouted over her shoulder, knowing full well that Higson hadn't a chance of keeping up. She glanced back at her friend and giggled again. Higson was not what one would call "handsome," but his face was kind and gentle with a ready smile. He was smiling now. Even though he was shorter than Carling, his body was strong and toned from a life in the outdoors. As was typical, his clothing was well worn and a tad on the dirty side.

To give her friend a chance to catch up, Carling decided to hide in the branches of a pine tree, intending to surprise Higson when he approached. She leaped up and grabbed a branch. With the agility that only she of all the

Duende possessed, she swung her unusually long legs up and over the branch, then settled herself among the pine needles and waited, snickering with delight.

Suddenly she was aware of the sound of laughter. She pivoted around on the branch and peeked between the pine boughs in the direction from which the sound was coming. A short distance away, in a meadow filled with sunshine and flowers, five young Centaur fillies were romping and dancing. They had made themselves necklaces of flowers and woven even more flowers into their long, flowing tails. As they played, they laughed and sang Centaur songs that were unfamiliar to Carling.

Carling grasped the trunk of the tree and watched with delight as the young and beautiful Centaurs played. She pushed away a wave of envy as she watched their beautiful quadruped bodies rear and buck across the flowers. Their delicate legs carried them swiftly as they raced around the meadow, long hair and tails flowing out behind them. The fillies' bodies were different colors; while one was chestnut, another was palomino, and the rest were white or bay. Each young filly's human torso rose out of her horse body at the withers. Soft flowing tunics covered their upper bodies, mimicking the filly's hair as they streamed out behind them.

"Carling!" Higson called from just beneath the tree in which Carling had secreted herself. "Where are you?"

"Shhhhh! I'm up here," she whispered. Without saying another word, she motioned for her friend to climb up and join her.

It wasn't as easy for him to make it to the branch, so Carling reached down and pulled him up beside her. Higson's face told her he didn't really like heights. He clung tightly to the trunk of the tree, one leg draped on either side of the branch. "What are you doing up here?" he asked, his voice filled with irritation.

Carling put a finger to her lips, then pushed aside the branches. "Look," she whispered.

The two friends sat in the tree, mesmerized by the scene in front of them. They had seen Centaurs on several occasions when the stallions and mares of the nearby herd of Centaurs came into the village of Duenton on market day. Even the Centaurs, skilled in so many ways, appreciated the artistry of Duende weaving, metalwork, pottery, and woodworking. The Duende, on the other hand, respected the gentle giants for their kindness and wisdom. Carling often watched them with admiration even as she felt intimidated by their size. She appreciated how they were always kind and friendly to her mother as they negotiated for cloth and rugs and other handwoven textiles.

But Carling had never seen young Centaurs, and certainly never seen them at play. This was something of a surprise to her. She had assumed they were all the serious and stately creatures she had always seen in her village. She found herself giggling and laughing with them.

Carling and Higson had been watching from their perch for nigh on a half hour when, suddenly, from the far side of the meadow, a group of dark and dirty Centaur stallions dashed into the center of the dancing fillies. With one or two of the intruders per young filly, they had no problem scooping them up in their hairy arms as easily as a child picks up a kitten. The fillies' singing turned to screaming as they struggled to get away from their captors. Using their delicate fists, they beat on the chests of their attackers. Their long legs kicked and pushed. But, being much smaller and weaker and greatly outnumbered, the fillies had no chance of getting away.

Carling gasped. Without any hesitation, she pulled her bow off her shoulder and reached behind her to retrieve an arrow from the leather quiver. Stiffening her left arm, she secured the nock on the bow string, pulled back, and released her grip on the arrow. The arrow zipped through the air and struck the furthest Centaur in the shoulder. With a yelp of pain, he dropped the young filly he was clutching to the ground. "What the...? Who shot me?" he yelled at the top of his oversized lungs.

All of the other Centaurs stopped and turned. Carling, confident that she was well hidden in the branches of the tree, reached over her shoulder and pulled another arrow from her quiver. Before she had it notched, another arrow whizzed past her and landed in the chest of another Centaur.

Carling turned toward Higson. "You don't get all the fun," her friend said, a big smile on his face.

Soon, two more arrows emerged from the trees that bordered the meadow and found their marks in the chests and arms of more of the would-be captors. More cries of pain and Centaur curse words filled the warm spring air of the field. Soon, all of the Centaur stallions were shouting and running for the far side of the meadow from which they had come. Two who'd tried to hold onto a filly during their escape soon let go of their captives as Duende arrows pierced their own shoulder blades. In short order, all the evil Centaurs had disappeared into the forest.

The five fillies remained on the ground, weeping. Carling and Higson leaped from their hiding place in the pine tree and dashed into the meadow. Carling ran up to the nearest filly and knelt on the ground beside her. "Are you alright?" she said, trying to catch her breath.

Sniffling loudly, the young chestnut Centaur turned her beautiful face toward Carling. "Are you the one who saved us?"

"Yes. We saw the whole thing from the forest," she said, motioning with her head in the direction from which they had come.

The filly put her delicate arms around Carling and wept.

Higson ran to check on the other fillies. One by one, they all gathered in a circle around Carling. One, a lovely palomino whose body shone like gold and whose white tresses and flowing tail reflected the sunlight like jewels, stepped forward. She spoke for all of her friends when she said, "Dear Duende, I am Tibbals, the daughter of the lead stallion of the Minsheen herd. What are your names?"

"I am Carling, from the village of Duenton."

"And I am Higson, her friend, also from the village of Duenton."

All of the fillies acknowledged the introduction with a nod of their heads and a swish of their tails. Tibbals continued, still brushing tears from her cheeks. "We cannot thank you enough for saving us from those beasts. My father will hear about your heroism, and our entire herd will be at your service whenever you are in need, from this day forth."

"But who were those Centaurs?" asked Carling.

"They must have been from the Heilodius herd. That group of Centaurs has separated itself from the others of our kind. They desire to rule the entire land of Crystonia and all races of the land. They are willing to do whatever it takes to secure the throne. I have no idea why they would try to abduct us, unless they planned to hold us for ransom."

At this, several of the other fillies burst into tears once again, their long hair draping over their pretty faces, their delicate shoulders shaking as they sobbed. Carling and Higson did their best to console them. Suddenly, the seriousness of the situation pierced Carling's heart. She had never done anything heroic in her life, and yet she had done this without a thought for herself. The fear and tension she had been holding inside needed a release. She wrapped her arms around Tibbals and burst into tears as well.

Higson looked from one crying female to another, as if unsure what to do. Finally, he just sat down on the grass and waited.

All of this was observed by eight burly and injured Centaurs from the cover of the far trees. The largest of the beasts clenched his jaw and ground his teeth as he pulled an arrow from his shoulder and rubbed his wound. His chest heaved and his breathing was so loud, it almost sounded like angry snorting. An animal-like growl arose from his throat as the Centaur scratched his greasy hair with the bloody tip of the arrow. Snapping the arrow in two, he threw its pieces to the ground, turned, and galloped away through the forest, followed by the others.

CHAPTER 6

Sixteen Years and One Day

THE DAY AFTER CARLING'S birthday, a contingent of Centaurs sent from the Minsheen herd, led by their lead stallion, Manti, walked majestically into the village square of Duenton. They wore elegant brocade vests on their chests and red capes that flowed from their shoulders down their backs to their croups. The hair of their heads was short, but their tails were long and glossy. The muscles on their arms bulged with strength, making them look like they had been sculpted from stone. Their shiny hooves clattered on the few cobblestone sections of the street. They stopped in front of the fountain that provided the villagers with their water supply.

Carling, was supposed to spend the morning weaving. Instead she was secretly reading a book she had borrowed titled *Heads and Tails Above the Rest: Why Centaurs Make the Best Leaders*. She jerked her head up at the first sound of hoof beats, tucked her book under the pillow of her bed and dashed out the door of her family cottage. Duende all over the village emerged from their homes and shops.

All eyes followed their every movement. Silence filled the square as though each Duende feared interrupting what felt to everyone to be a magical moment.

In a booming voice laced with obvious affection, the largest of all the group of Centaurs addressed the quickly gathering crowd. "Dear villagers of Duenton," he said, "I am Manti, the lead stallion of the Minsheen Herd. There are among you two heroes whom we have come to honor this day."

Whispers were exchanged between villagers as they looked back and forth at one another, wondering what this could possibly be about. Some leaned forward in anticipation. All except Carling and Higson, who stood together in the doorway of Carling's home, tried to get as close to the magnificent Centaur as they dared.

"Would the Duende by the names of Carling and Higson please step forward?" requested Manti.

The two friends looked at each other, their mouths forming grimaces more than smiles. Neither of the teenagers had told their parents what took place the day before, not sure how such news would be received. Now the entire village would learn at the same time. Clutching one another's hand, they made their way slowly through the crowd and stepped up to the Centaur. The stallion towered over them. Carling and Higson would have been a bit frightened if Manti hadn't leaned down and extended his arms to them in welcome. His handsome face beamed with admiration as he looked at them and smiled.

"So this is the lovely Carling. I was told to look for the violet eyes. You are as beautiful as my daughter said."

Carling blushed and glanced away.

"And this is the gallant Higson. It is such a pleasure to meet such a brave lad as you."

Now it was Higson's turn to blush.

Manti returned his attention to the crowd of Duende. "These two youngsters are heroes. I want all of you to know that you should be very proud of them."

Murmurs expressing curiosity rippled through the gathering of villagers.

"Yesterday," the stallion continued, "five of our fillies were frolicking in a meadow between our home on the sides of Mount Dashmoore and your village in this lovely valley. A band of evil Centaurs from the Heilodius herd attempted to abduct them. These two Duende, brave and skilled as they are, saved them from a horrible fate."

Cheers and shouts of congratulations mixed with questions arose from the villagers. Carling searched until she found her mother, Saleen, who stood silently at the edge of the crowd, her mouth agape. Their eyes met. Carling wasn't sure how to read what was written there, but it didn't look anything like joy or pride or anything good. The young girl simply smiled weakly and looked downward, then pressed her fist to her lips as she felt the hurt well up inside of her. She had never kept anything from her mother. She barely heard Manti's next statement.

"Tomorrow," he continued, "the Minsheen herd will hold a celebration, and we would like Carling and Higson to be our guests of honor."

A gasp went up from the crowd. Never in the history of the Duende had one of their kind been invited to a village inhabited by Centaurs. This was an unspeakable honor, one that would go down in the Duende history books.

Eyes wide, Carling and Higson looked at each other, then lifted their faces to look up at Manti. Carling's face wore an expression that fell somewhere between embarrassment and pride—neither of which was familiar to her.

"We would be honored to come," she whispered, speaking for both of them.

Manti smiled. "Wonderful! We will send two Centaurs to fetch you tomorrow when the sun reaches its zenith."

The beautiful Centaurs reared up in the air, waved farewell, and galloped out of the village. Everyone watched them go, no doubt feeling just a tinge of jealousy. Slowly the villagers left the town square, several of them stopping first to talk with Carling and Higson, and soon everyone had returned to their homes and shops...except Saleen. She remained in the same spot, as though her feet were nailed to the ground. Still she said nothing.

When the Duende who had surrounded Carling to ask questions finally dispersed, the girl stepped up to her mother.

"Mother?"

"What is this all about, Carling?" Saleen asked. "What happened?"

Carling proceeded to recount the previous day's events to her mother, who listened with her brow knotted in apparent concern. When her daughter had finished, Saleen said, "And just when did you learn to shoot a bow and arrow?"

CHAPTER 7

The City of Minsheen

THE NEXT DAY, AT high noon, two beautiful Centaurs cantered into the village of Duenton. A large crowd of villagers had gathered in the town square in anticipation of their arrival. Saleen was not one of them.

When the two Centaurs arrived, Carling and Higson were waiting. Carling had been so excited, she hadn't slept a wink all night. She'd put on her new birthday dress early in the morning, the one her mother had lovingly made. The purple fabric was infused with specks of golden thread that made her violet eyes even more vibrant. Her auburn hair fell in soft waves around her face. The effect was stunning. The beautiful young Duende then rushed through her chores and finished them early as her mother fixed her a breakfast of biscuits and fruit but said nothing. Carling felt badly that her mother was so upset, but that didn't dampen her enthusiasm for what the day promised to bring.

Now Carling was standing beside Higson in the center of the town as two Centaurs slid to a stop on the mud, the dirt surface of the square having been moistened by the previous night's spring rains. "Carling and Higson," the smaller of the two said by way of greeting. "We have come to take you to the great city of the Minsheen herd. Please mount up." The speaker bowed by dropping one knee to the ground, a very humbling position for a proud Centaur to take. Carling climbed up on his dapple gray back. The taller Centaur, chestnut in color, clasped Higson's forearm and swung him up to his back as though he weighed no more than a bird.

Both Duende grabbed a hold of the leather belts that were buckled around the Centaurs' waists to hold in the red shirts they wore over their chests.

"Are you settled?" the larger Centaur asked.

Both of the Duende nodded, too excited to speak, while the crowd of villagers cheered.

The Centaurs pivoted on their hindquarters and cantered out of the village.

Saleen watched silently from the window of her little home, her hands clutched to her chest. She pursed her lips and sighed deeply. Tears filled her eyes as she watched her little girl ride away. Clearly a feeling of foreboding encompassed her. The little mother turned from the window, cradled her face in her hands, and sobbed.

Carling dared to look back at her village just before they entered the forest. She knew not that she would never see her village so sweet and idyllic again.

According to Duende history, no member of their race had ever been in a Centaur city, let alone as an honored guest. But it wasn't history that Carling was thinking about now as she held tightly to the Centaur she was riding. She was thinking about staying on her mount. When the Centaurs picked up speed, she let go of the belt and wrapped her arms around her escort's waist, her fingers interlocking over the golden buttons on his red shirt.

According to Duende records, no one of their race had ever ridden on the back of a Centaur, either. She was truly making history today! As they galloped along, the young Duende was filled with excitement and a little anxiety. She had never moved as quickly as she was moving now. She kept herself from looking down at the ground as it whizzed by to avoid getting nauseous. Carling glanced over at Higson and noticed the set of his jaw. She figured he must be feeling the same way. Gradually she felt herself getting more confident and comfortable and let her body move with the power beneath her. A smile filled her face as she let the wind of heaven flow through her auburn hair.

They cantered through forest and glen, moving rapidly toward Mount Dashmoore. The fresh green leaves smelled sweet, the spring sun warmed their faces. At one point, they crossed the meadow that had been the scene of the attempted abduction.

Once they crossed the flower-filled field, nothing looked familiar. This was new territory for Carling. She wondered if Higson had ever traveled this far from the village on his hunting trips. She made a mental note to ask him later, when she had both feet safely on the ground!

Gradually, Carling began to feel a bit more comfortable on the back of the Centaur. Her body began to move with the rhythm of the cantering animal as his shoulders reached forward and his haunches pushed from behind.

She found herself loving the feeling, everything about it, from the warmth of his body next to her legs to the wind brushing her auburn hair back from her glowing face. When she looked over at Higson, she noticed that he, too, seemed to be feeling more confident. His mouth, which had been set in a grim, straight line, was now turning up just slightly at the corners.

On and on they went, weaving between trees in the dense forest, jumping over rapidly moving streams, following along the base of red stone cliffs they called the Hogback. Birds and squirrels scolded them from the treetops, upset that the tranquility of the forest was being disturbed.

Eventually, the ground started to slope upward and the Centaurs slowed to a smooth trot. Not much later, the forest opened up and the two Duende were treated to their first view of the City of Minsheen. Carling's hand flew to her mouth and her eyes opened wide in wonder. The city ahead was completely unlike her little village of plaster-and-beam huts. This city sparkled with tall white towers, glistening windows, and roofs made of gold. Vines covered with flowers crept up the sides of the elegant buildings. Carved doors at the city gates stood open, welcoming all to enter.

The Centaurs slowed to a walk as they passed through the gates. Once in the city, Centaurs of all ages waved and cheered as Carling and Higson were carried through the streets. The two Duende loosened their grips on the Centaur's bodies and waved in return. Both their faces were red, reflecting either embarrassment or excitement or, perhaps, a bit of both.

Their escorts carried Carling and Higson toward a large building in the center of the city, then walked up a gently sloping ramp that opened at a raised city square, a city square that put the little one in the village of Duenton to shame. All around were marble sculptures of Centaurs in various elegant poses. The Centaurs' beautiful bodies seemed made for imitation in any art form, unlike the squat little bodies of the Duende.

The buildings, both homes and shops, that surrounded the square were also works of art. They were all white and sparkled as though diamonds were imbedded in them. Each doorframe was beautifully carved with floral designs and surrounded a brightly painted door. Tall, leaded-glass windows were set in the walls. Round towers graced the corners. The effect was magical.

Just as the two guests were brought to the center of the square, five beautiful fillies of different colors cantered up to them, their dainty hooves, polished with glitter, tapping lightly on the brick surface of the central plaza. With excited giggles, they reached up their slender arms and pulled Carling and Higson off their mounts. They embraced the two Duende tightly.

"You're here at last! We thought you would never arrive," gushed Tibbals. She placed a garland of flowers over each of their heads.

Her friends surrounded them on all sides and chatted excitedly.

"How was your ride?"

"Do you like Minsheen?"

"We have a fabulous feast planned for you!"

Carling and Higson looked from one to the other, feeling a bit overwhelmed.

Tibbals clasped Carling's hand. "Follow me. My father and mother are waiting for your arrival."

They walked toward a large building at the far end of the square. This building was more ornate than any of the others. A long row of wide steps, built for easy accommodation by a four-legged Centaur, led up to the front entrance. It was up this staircase that the two Duende were escorted, having been joined by several other young fillies and colts.

One of the young colts rushed ahead of the others and reached out to open the door. Bowing deeply, he motioned them inside with a sweep of his arm. The fillies giggled like girls of any race would.

Carling stepped into the foyer of the building with her mouth agape at the beauty all around her. An enormous chandelier was suspended from the center of the domed ceiling. The walls were hung with large oil portraits of Centaurs. Music filled the room. The air smelled of fresh pine and roses. It was pure perfection. She had never seen anything so elegant.

Higson stopped in place. "Wow."

Carling giggled at her friend's reaction. She felt the same way but hoped she could express it a bit more eloquently. She turned to Tibbals. "This is gorgeous. What building is this?"

"Our government building. You might call it City Hall. We call it Minsheen Palace. This is where my father, the current leader of the city, holds his meetings."

At that moment, a trumpet fanfare filled the air, echoing around the domed chamber. Manti and several other Centaurs, mares and stallions, entered the foyer. One of the mares left the group and trotted up to Carling and Higson. She bent down and scooped both of them into a tight embrace.

"Oh, my darlings. How can a mother such as I ever express her heartfelt gratitude? You saved my beloved daughter. I have nightmares and nightstallions just thinking about what could have been, had you not fought off those awful criminals." She let go of them and blew her nose on a dainty handkerchief. She smiled down at them. "You are my heroes."

Tibbals stepped forward. "Carling and Higson, this is my mother, Tamah, the lead mare of the city."

"It is a pleasure to meet you," said Carling with a curtsey. "But we didn't do anything that anyone else wouldn't have done."

Manti stepped up. He was beaming at the young Duende, his arms open wide. "On the contrary, my dear young Duende. Many of both our races would have stood back in fear of the evil Heilodius herd. Others would not have had the skills to shoot them without harming our fillies. By the way, where did you two learn to handle a bow and arrow like that? From what Tibbals has told me, you are accomplished sharp shooters who could challenge any of our soldiers!"

Carling turned to Higson. "Higson taught me. He's a great hunter. We've been practicing for a long time."

"I never had to use my arrows on a Centaur before," said Higson as he dropped his eyes. "And really, it was Carling who should get all the credit. She sent off the first arrow without a moment's hesitation."

Tibbals' mother brushed aside their humble responses. "Oh, you are both much too modest. But the trait suits you well. Now it's time to celebrate with a feast," gushed Tamah.

The mare turned and led the large group into a banquet hall, where an enormous table was set with china, crystal, and silver. The chairs pulled up to the table were specially designed to hold a Centaur's horse-like elongated body. Carling and Higson were escorted to the front of the room. A large chair was pulled out for them.

"I'm sorry about the chairs," giggled Tibbals. "They really are much too big for you."

"Oh, don't worry," said Carling with a smile. "We can just sit together on the edge."

Carling and Higson made themselves comfortable as they propped themselves on the front of the lounge-like chair. Their feet dangled over the edge; not even their toes could reach the floor.

Centaurs dressed in gold shirts and white aprons brought out platter after platter of delicious food. Roast beef, venison, pheasant, and pork were passed from guest to guest, starting with Carling and Higson. Fruits and vegetables and baskets of rolls followed. Beverage glasses were kept full of carrot juice and apple juice. Carling laughed as Higson filled and consumed plate after plate.

As the meal was served and eaten, they were entertained by an orchestra composed of string instruments played with bows made of horse-hair. Happy chatter and boisterous laughter filled the room. The entire event was unlike anything Carling and her friend had ever seen.

After a dessert of oatmeal cookies and carrot cake, Manti asked that all the goblets be refilled with apple juice. He then stood before the crowd at the table. Smiling broadly, he addressed the guests. "Mares and Stallions and our Duende guests of honor, I would like to propose a toast. I, the lead stallion of the City of Minsheen, declare that from this day forth, we will be the guardians and protectors of all Duende!"

A cheer went up from the guests and goblets were emptied. Carling and Higson beamed.

Unfortunately, what was the most wonderful day of Carling's life was soon to become the worst.

CHAPTER 8

The Attack

THE SUN WAS LOW in the sky when Carling and Higson, riding on the broad backs of their Centaur mounts, neared their village. Had there been more daylight, they might have seen the smoke earlier. As it was, they were nearly to Duenton before they smelled the smoke and heard the wailing of mourning villagers. As they emerged from the forest, Carling's hand flew to her mouth. She could not believe what her eyes were telling her. Her entire village was in flames. Each little house and shop was burning and on its way to being destroyed. Flames lapped out the doorways and broken windows. Roofs collapsed. Amid the rubble of many structures, only stone chimneys remained standing.

Carling screamed and leaped from the back of her Centaur. As soon as her feet touched the ground, she started running toward her home.

Higson was right behind her. "Carling! Wait! Wait for me!"

She was not conscious of him calling out to her, nor of the Centaurs cantering beside her. She wove between burning buildings, her lungs aching and her eyes stinging. Up ahead, she could just barely make out flames coming from her home.

As she neared the burning house, the village smithy, Ashtic, caught her in his arms. "Stop, Carling. Don't go in there. There is nothing you can do."

She struggled and then, adrenaline giving her strength, began hitting his chest with her fists. "Let go! Let go of me!"

The Centaurs and Higson came up beside her.

"Get on my back," said one. "I will carry you swiftly through the flames and keep you safe. We will search for your parents together."

"I'm coming, too," said Higson as he swung his leg up on the Centaur's back and pulled Carling up after him.

The Centaur galloped toward the burning house. One side of the cottage had already collapsed. He chose that place to enter the wreckage that had once been a home. With a powerful push from his haunches, the Centaur lifted his body over the fallen timbers and landed in what had been the main room of the house. Here, Saleen's loom now stood as a twisted, blackened skeleton.

The smoke and heat made it both difficult to see and to breathe. With hearts pounding and hands covering mouths and noses, the three rescuers scanned the room. Large holes were open in the ceiling, through which pungent smoke and hot, curling flames were now escaping. Sooty shingles littered the floor. Timbers that had once supported the walls and roof were strewn across the entire area, signaling the extreme danger all of them were in by being there.

A breath of wind coming from the gaping hole that had once been a wall cleared the room for just a moment—just long enough for Carling to see her father. He was lying on his stomach, his legs and feet twisted unnaturally backward. She jumped off the Centaur and ran to him, her heart in her throat. She knew instantly that they were too late.

Higson pushed her aside as he knelt beside her father. "Find your mother."

Carling seemed to be functioning as though she was not even conscious of what she was doing, like a puppet whose strings were being manipulated by someone else. She hurried through the burning room. A soft noise caught her attention. Where it was coming from she could not tell, but her instincts caused her to turn toward the kitchen. She crawled through a former doorway that was now partially blocked by a collapsed doorframe. There, lying on the floor among broken dishes and twisted metal pans, moaning in pain, was her dear mother.

Carling shouted. "Mother! Centaur, Higson, come quickly! My mother's in here and she's alive." The Centaur crashed through a partial wall and scooped Saleen up in his arms.

As he did so, Saleen squirmed and with a weak arm stretched down, blood flowing down to the tip of her finger, pointed toward the floorboards. With tremendous effort she coughed and choked out the words. "There...in there."

"Hush, mother. We need to get you out of here," Carling said.

Carling followed the Centaur out of the house, all of them coughing and gasping, their lungs and eyes seeking the fresh night air.

But Saleen seemed agitated. Too weak to move more than the tiniest bit, she kept pointing back toward the house. "Carling," she whispered through parched lips, her eyes open only slightly. "Carling," she whispered again. The Centaur lowered her gently to the ground.

Carling bent down, tears flowing freely down her cheeks. "I'm here, Mother."

A frail hand reached up and pulled Carling by the collar of her birthday dress, which was now blackened with smoke. "Carling...."

"Mother, don't talk. You are too weak."

A slight shake of the head and a tiny tug on the collar brought Carling closer to her face. "Under the kitchen floor...." A violent series of coughs followed and Carling gasped when she saw blood flowing out of her mother's mouth.

"Mother, please...."

"Under the kitchen floor...for you...." Saleen's hand fell to her chest, and Carling's mother closed her eyes for the last time.

CHAPTER 9

The Work of Evil

In a pitiful voice, Carling cried out, "Motherrrrrr!" Her pleading cry was so loud it was heard throughout the streets of the little village, bouncing back and forth as though echoing off cold, stone canyon walls. She collapsed over her mother's body, wrapping her arms around her, refusing to let her go.

Gradually the flames throughout the village dissipated. Glowing orange embers floated skyward in lazy swirls. The little residents of the village of Duenton crept out of their hiding places to assess the damage and see what they could do to help one another. Carling remained on her knees beside her mother, her hands covering her face as she cried uncontrollably. Higson knelt beside her and put his arms around his best friend.

The two Centaurs that had brought Carling and Higson home circulated around the village, trying to determine what had happened here. Everywhere the story was the same:

A band of Centaurs, dressed in black with masks over their faces, had stormed into the village in broad daylight, demanding to know the location of the two Duende teens who had saved the fillies. Everyone had refused to speak to them...until they started setting homes and businesses on fire. Then Saleen stepped forward.

"It is I you are seeking," she said to the apparent leader.

"You?" he scoffed. "You are not a teenager."

"I am responsible for what my daughter did."

"Your daughter? Then tell me where she is."

"I cannot...will not do that."

The Centaur grabbed her by the throat. At that point, Carling's father attacked the Centaur with a shovel. Two other Centaurs pulled him off. They demanded to be shown the location of their home. When the girl was not found at their little cottage, both parents were severely beaten and left to die. The house was set on fire.

The evil Centaurs ran out of the village, promising to return one day and finish what they had come to do...execute their revenge on Carling and Higson.

The Centaurs from Minsheen called the villagers together. "My dear friends, we will help you."

"You brought this upon us!" shouted one Duende woman as she clutched her weeping child to her breast.

"Yes," responded another woman. "We never had any problems until those two children saved your fillies."

"Now look what's happened. Our homes, our stores, our entire village is destroyed!" several shouted at once.

"And Saleen and her husband are dead," wailed a more compassionate villager before burying her face in her scarf and sobbing.

The Centaurs nodded. "This all appears to be true. We certainly never foresaw such a terrible result of Carling's and Higson's heroism."

A few Duende scoffed at the word "heroism."

One of the Centaurs held up his hand. "But I promise you that, with the exception of Carling's parents, whom we cannot bring back to life, we will put all things right. We will help you rebuild your village, and we will provide guards for your town. You will be safe under our care. We promise."

CHAPTER 10

Finding the Breastplate

CARLING SPENT A SLEEPLESS night in Higson's home, one of the few structures left untouched due to the fact that it was located quite a distance away from the actual village and hidden in the forest. Her grief was overwhelming, and the pain of her broken heart sent poison throughout her body. She had always felt safe and greatly loved in her parents' home. Now they were gone, and all things that had seemed secure and permanent had disappeared with them.

Higson's mother did her best to comfort the girl, offering her warm milk and honey, a soft blanket, and tight hugs. But nothing really worked. Carling was distraught and blamed herself for all that had happened to both her parents and her village. One minute she'd been a celebrated hero, and the next she'd become a reviled villain. She wanted to run. But to where could she run? She wanted to hide. But hide where and from what? How can you hide from your own feelings, your own fears? They fill you up completely and grow with every breath you take.

"Why did I ever shoot that first arrow?" she asked aloud, her violet eyes dull with pain.

"Because you saw some young fillies in danger," said Higson's mother, wrapping her arms tightly around the girl.

"You did the right thing, Carling," said Higson's father as he patted her shoulder. "The evil acts of the Heilodius Centaurs prove what kind of villains they are. I just wish I had been able to fight them myself. Your father did his best, but we Duende are no match for such big, strong creatures."

Tears ran down Carling's cheeks, leaving a salty crust on her fair skin.

The next day brought both sunshine and, as promised, a large crew of Centaurs from the City of Minsheen in the foothills of Mount Dashmoore. Manti was at the lead. They came with tools of all sorts to help clean up the devastation and start the rebuilding. Their large size and great strength enabled them to get much more done in far less time than the little Duende could possibly have hoped to accomplish on their own.

Carling was determined to do what she could to help, even though Higson and his parents pleaded with her to stay in their home and rest. "I cannot just sit here while everyone else works. I will do all I can to make up for the trouble I've caused."

Carling hoped that keeping busy would help her keep her mind off the pain she was feeling. So Carling and Higson, along with his parents, went into the village, tools in hand. They headed first to the town square, where the City Hall was the only building undamaged. Carling intentionally avoiding returning to her home. She was afraid to face it, afraid she couldn't go inside, and afraid she couldn't stay out.

At one point, Carling stopped and just stared at the destruction all around. Higson stopped beside her, taking her hand in his. The smell of damp, charred wood filled the air. Piles of rubbish filled the streets. Sorrow filled every heart. Many of the pine trees stood bare of needles, their branches looking like black skeletons. Gone were the spring flowers. Gone the lovely little homes and shops. Several wisps of smoke still curled upward, like snakes arising from a charmer's basket. Carling took a deep breath, clenched her teeth, brushed her hair back from her face, lifted her chin, and walked down the street.

The four of them joined a crew working on the little school. As they pulled out burned desks and books, Higson asked her, "Carling, what was your mother saying about the kitchen floor?"

"Hum?" said Carling as she gathered up some hats and coats from the lost and found, the odor of smoke emanating from their fabric.

"You know. She said something about the kitchen floor...under the kitchen floor."

Carling looked at him with her brows knotted, thinking he was crazy. "I don't know what you're talking about."

"Carling, don't you remember? Just before she died, she said there was something for you under the kitchen floor."

"No. I don't remember anything like that," she responded as she turned away to hide the tears that were stinging the backs of her violet eyes.

"I heard her say that. I think we should go to your house and check before the work crews get there."

Carling stood upright, her back to Higson. "I don't think I can go back there."

"Would you like me to go?"

"No. I think you must have misunderstood my mother. What could possibly be under the kitchen floor? She was dying, probably hallucinating...she didn't know what she was saying."

Higson put his hand on his friend's shoulder and spoke to the back of her head. "That could be true. But what if it isn't? What if there *is* something she really wanted you to have? Maybe a family heirloom, a special gift she had been saving...I don't know. I just think we should check."

Carling lowered her shoulders and sighed. Slowly she turned around to face Higson. "All right. We'll go. But don't be surprised if nothing's there."

The two Duende walked to the wreckage that was once Carling's home. It smelled like a campfire after a rain. Little towers of steam still arose from hotspots throughout the house. They scrambled through the wreckage and into the remains of the kitchen, where Higson began clearing away a pile of rubble. Carling joined him with little enthusiasm and even less energy. Some pieces of debris were so heavy, it took both of them to move them. Finally, the floor was cleared enough to reveal the little rug that was so familiar to Carling. She dropped to her knees and scooped the rug up in her arms, clutching it to her chest. She pressed it to her face, hoping to breathe in the familiar odors of her mother's kitchen. But all she could smell was smoke. She threw the rug down as a stab of fear entered her heart and spread throughout her body. She knew not what the future would bring, and the thought of facing it without her parents terrified her. She started sobbing.

Higson stood beside her and waited.

After several minutes of crying, Carling sniffed loudly. She wiped her puffy eyes with her sleeve.

"I'm sorry," Carling said softly.

"Don't be. I think I can understand."

Carling felt a surge of anger fill her. "No! You can't! You've never had your parents killed because of something you did."

As soon as she said it, she wished she hadn't. She could see the pain her words had caused reflected in his eyes.

"Forgive me, Higson. I didn't mean that. And you certainly don't deserve that."

"It's okay," Higson responded quietly. He knelt beside his friend and wrapped his arms around her. Carling felt herself melt against him as she let him absorb some of her pain.

Eventually, Higson brought her back to the task at hand. "Are you ready to see what your mother left you?"

Carling sighed. "I guess so," she said, still doubting there was anything there and not really sure she wanted to see it if there was. Additionally, she was quite sure she didn't want to leave Higson's embrace.

Slowly, she straightened and pushed away from her friend. She looked down at the dirty floor beneath her feet. Built into the floor of rough-hewn boards was a door. The wood grain matched so perfectly, however, that it was nearly impossible to detect. Two small holes chiseled into one end provided a handhold. Carling was sure she had never seen the door before. Hesitantly, she reached down, put her fingers in the handhold, and pulled. The boards creaked and groaned as they scraped against one another but then grudgingly cooperated. Higson helped her move the door to one side.

Both young Duende got on their knees and peeked into the black hole. They waited for their eyes to adjust to the darkness. As they did so, an object became visible. About two feet down in the dark, damp, musty-smelling hole, an oddly shaped package could just barely be seen. Carling felt herself freeze in place.

Higson must have sensed her hesitation. He patted her on the arm and said, "Do you want me to get it out?"

Carling nodded.

Higson moved onto his stomach and reached down into the hole. His arms were just barely long enough to reach the burlap-covered package. He wrapped his fingers around its edges and lifted it out of the hole. The weight of it caused his muscles to strain. The young Duende set the heavy package on the charred remains of the kitchen table. Immediately, the table collapsed, crashing to the floor, taking the package with it.

"Oh, no!" cried Carling.

Higson grabbed the package and placed it in a fairly clear space on the floor. "Sorry about that, Carling," he said sheepishly. He bowed low and with a swoop of his arm said, "Your inheritance, my lady. You need to do the honors of opening it."

Carling moved over, crawling across the rough, dirty floorboards on her hands and knees. The burlap wrapping was tied together with twine and secured with a bow in the center. She reached out her slender hand, noticing how it trembled, and untied the bow. With the twine out of the way, she clasped the folded edges of the burlap and parted them.

In that instant, both Carling and Higson fell backward as though pushed by an unseen force. A bright beam of light shot up to the sagging ceiling from a strange silver object. A soft hum was heard coming from the beam of light.

As the two Duende gazed at the pulsating beam, a tall, thin figure materialized before them.

"Carling," the figure said in little more than a whisper.

Realizing that her mouth was hanging open, she quickly shut it. For some unknown reason, Carling felt remarkably safe in the presence of this mysterious, magical stranger who was calling her name. While Higson remained frozen in place, Carling slowly rose to her feet to greet the visitor.

"Carling," he repeated, his voice sounding like a choir singing.

"It is I," said Carling. "Who are you?"

"My name is Vidente. I am the Wizard of Crystonia."

Carling cocked her head to one side, searching her memory to see if she'd ever heard of such a being. Nothing came to mind. "I know nothing about you."

"That is not a surprise. Few in Crystonia do."

"Why have you come to me?" she asked.

"You have been chosen to perform a great work."

Carling raised her eyebrows, wrinkling her forehead in surprise. "What is it that you desire of me?" she responded meekly.

"You have been foreordained to become the queen of Crystonia."

"Queen?" Carling whispered, her heart pounding, her palms suddenly sweating.

The stranger who called himself "Vidente" nodded. "For far too long, your land has been without a righteous ruler. You, my child, must become that leader."

"I'm sorry to question you, sir, but how is that to be as I am still but a child? I know not the ways of the world. I have barely left the confines of my own little village. And now I am alone in the world with no one to guide me. My parents have been killed...." She paused. "But you knew that, didn't you?"

Vidente nodded, his eyes filled with both sorrow and compassion. "Yes, I know what happened to your parents. You must do whatever you can to ensure that no others are left orphaned by the evil forces that are moving across the kingdom."

"But I ask you again, oh Wizard, how can I be the queen of this land?"

The stranger bent down and picked up the silver breastplate. The highly polished metal sparkled in his hands. "This breastplate will be the source of your power and protection. But it is incomplete."

The Wizard pointed to the four empty circles on the breastplate. "In order for you to become a righteous leader, the kind of ruler that this land needs, you must fulfill an important assignment. Each of these holes holds a sacred stone that carries marvelous powers and will endow you with the skills and traits you will need. I call them 'The Stones of Light'." Pointing to each of the holes one by one he said, "This space is for the Stone of Mercy, this the Stone of Courage, this the Stone of Integrity, and finally," he pointed to the circle in the center, "the Stone of Wisdom."

He smiled kindly at the young Duende. "You, my little Carling, must gather each stone and put it in its place on the breastplate before you will be worthy to rule the land of Crystonia."

Carling could feel her heart pounding in her chest. Her breath was shallow. Her mind was racing, filled with doubts, questions, and, yes, fears. She choked out one word: "Alone?"

The Wizard's eyes sparkled with understanding. He glanced over at Higson, who had remained in a trance-like state during their entire conversation. "Higson, my young lad, you may join us now."

Higson blinked and shook his head as though awakening from a deep sleep. "W-what?" he stammered.

Suddenly appearing to notice Vidente for the first time, he jerked his head upward. "Who are you?"

Carling stepped over to him. "It's alright, Higson. This is the Wizard of Crystonia. His name is Vidente."

The Wizard dipped his head in acknowledgement. Higson let his jaw drop open and just stared.

Vidente chuckled. "My dear Higson. Will you be Carling's companion as she fulfills an important assignment?"

With his mouth still hanging open and without even asking what the assignment was, Higson nodded, his head bobbing up and down as if on a string.

Vidente chuckled again. "That's my boy. A loyal friend, to be sure."

Turning back to Carling, he continued his instruction. "The first stone you are to find is the Stone of Mercy. The great eagle Baskus has been protecting it. You must find Baskus. He will give it to you."

Vidente stroked his long gray beard and studied Carling carefully. "I must warn you, however, there are powers of evil growing stronger and stronger across the land. Once it is known that the Silver Breastplate has been created and given to its rightful owner, every effort will be made to keep you from completing your mission. I fear that each stone will become more and more difficult to obtain. I advise you to keep your quest a secret from all except a carefully chosen few. You must understand that many others desire to obtain the throne for themselves. Now go. Go swiftly. "

Before Carling could even ask the questions that filled her head, Vidente disappeared.

"Vidente! Vidente! Don't go. I need your help," she called out in desperation.

There was no response. Vidente was gone, and the silver breastplate lay sparkling on the floor at her feet.

Left alone in the ruins of Carling's family home, the two Duende looked down at the silver breastplate. It continued to sparkle as though of its own internal light.

"Should I put it on?" Carling asked with both timidity and curiosity.

"I have the feeling you're supposed to," Higson said as he lifted the silver breastplate. Just as he did so, the breastplate dissolved in his hands and disappeared. Startled, Higson looked up into the surprised face of Carling. She stood before him, her arms outstretched, her torso covered with the silver breastplate.

"Well, I guess you didn't need my help," he said with a nervous chuckle.

Both of them were beginning to realize there was a power here they didn't understand, and certainly couldn't control. Carling's lips began to quiver and she could feel tears welling up in her eyes. There was magic here, and she knew instinctively to treat magic with caution.

"Yes, I do, Higson," she said. "I need your help now more than ever. I don't understand any of this, and I'm frightened."

"To tell you the truth, Carling," her friend said, "it scares me, too. It scares me a lot!"

CHAPTER 11

Adivino

THE OLD CENTAUR STOOD by his desk. He dipped his quill pen in the little bottle of ink and carefully formed the letters of the Centaur alphabet. Slowly and beautifully the words took shape under his hand, adding to the Centaurian history. Today, he was continuing the account of the conflict that was erupting between the Minsheen herd and the Heilodius herd. At one time, they had been united as a strong and beautiful race. But that had been when there was peace in the land. Those days were gone as the faction that desired to rule the land separated itself from the Minsheen. The Heilodius herd had taken upon themselves the name of the mountain from which the rightful ruler of the land would one day govern. But they, along with all the other races, had been unable to maintain control as they fought against the Cyclops and Ogres, who also desired to hold the throne of leadership atop Mount Heilodius.

The members of the Minsheen herd who continued to wait and watch for the promised bearer of the silver breastplate, the rightful ruler of the land, tried to remain out of the battles, taking up arms only when it was necessary to defend themselves. The Heilodius herd mocked and belittled them for putting their faith in myths and legends. The split in the Centaur race saddened the Minsheen as they watched their brothers participate in the conflict for power. It was a heartbreaking story that Adivino, the keeper of the records, was now writing.

The historian's pen suddenly stopped scratching on the scroll. "I've been expecting you, Vidente," Adivino said, having sensed the Wizard's presence without turning around.

"Ah, my old friend. I am glad to see you," responded Vidente warmly.

The Centaur turned and stepped forward, extending both arms. For a moment their hands touched, palm to palm, and Adivino felt a warm current flow through him.

"Is the queen beginning her quest?" he asked. "Is it time?"

"Yes. It is time," replied the Wizard, his voice lacking enthusiasm.

Adivino cocked his head. "Why so down in the mouth? I would think this was cause for celebration."

"I just worry that we may be placing too much on the shoulders of one so young."

"What would you have me do to assist her?" asked Adivino.

"I need two young, strong Centaurs to carry the future queen on her journeys."

The old Centaur nodded. "Do you need them for their speed, protection, or wisdom?"

"All of those qualities, Adivino. All of them."

"Will you at least tell me who the queen is that I may make the correct selection?"

"It is the Duende named Carling. And she will be accompanied by her friend Higson."

"A Duende?" Adivino was surprised. Quickly processing this new information, he nodded. "The Duende are a noble race to be sure. And Carling certainly seems to have the qualities of a leader. Though you are right; she is still so young..." He let the rest of his thought hang in the air while rubbing his ink-stained hands on his apron.

Gathering control of his thoughts, he said, "Yes. Yes, of course. That makes perfect sense. The brave and beautiful Carling. While I did not anticipate the queen would come from the Duende race, this makes perfect sense indeed. And Higson is a very impressive young man as well." He paused and gazed up toward the ceiling of his charming little cottage. "Well," he said after a time, "that tells me who I should send on this perilous journey."

The Quest Begins

THE NEXT MORNING, CARLING was awakened by the birds and squirrels scolding one another in the trees. The early morning sun was painting the eastern sky a bright pink. But none of nature's beauty around her stopped the memory of her parents' death from crushing her. The weight of it made her feel small, weak, insignificant. She pulled the blankets over her head to make a cocoon to shield her from the world. She remained there a long time.

Finally, getting her labored breathing and pounding heart under control, she stretched her tired body. Pushing back the blankets and turning her head, Carling let her gaze rest upon the silver breastplate, the object that filled her with such varied and extreme emotions. She had never imagined herself as anything but a weaver's daughter, a citizen of the village of Duenton. She had never desired power or riches or even the honors of men. She wanted nothing more than to continue the life into which she had been born...except, perhaps, a little more time to go hunting in the forest with Higson.

Now her life had completely changed. Her parents were gone and, in her mind, it was her fault. In addition, a Wizard had come into her life, telling her she was to become the queen of Crystonia. She continued gazing at the silver breastplate, the tangible proof that all of this was real. She couldn't just write it off as a very bad dream. But even in the presence of the breastplate, the sixteen-year-old Duende found the truth it reflected impossible to comprehend.

She tried to gather her thoughts and focus on the task at hand: to complete the queen's breastplate by finding the four stones of light. The Wizard named Vidente had given her information on just one of the stones, the Stone of Mercy. So, for today, that was what she needed to concentrate on. Yes, today was a new day in every way. Today, she needed to begin the quest to find the Stone of Mercy.

She grabbed her leather pack and began removing items she wouldn't need. The pack was old and well-worn and covered with streaks of black ash from the fire, a constant reminder of her sorrow. She grabbed her bow and quiver and hung them on the sides of her pack, in easy reach in case she needed them. She made a mental note to remind Higson to bring his weapon along as well.

The packing was completed quickly, for she had very little to take. Carling washed and dressed just as quickly. She paused and gazed at her reflection in the little mirror hanging on the wall. *Strange*, she thought as she brushed her wavy auburn hair, *I look just the same. But I certainly don't feel the same.*

She turned away from the mirror and stepped over to the breastplate. As soon as she reached down to pick it up, it opened along the sides of its own accord. Clearly, it knew its owner.

She placed it on her body. Carling felt a strange sensation as the breastplate melted against her and latched itself. Perhaps she felt taller, maybe a bit bolder, and clearly safer. However she chose to describe the feeling, she liked it. She caressed the silver carvings that now covered her body and smiled to herself.

The young Duende pulled herself out of her self-diagnosis long enough to cover the breastplate with a pale green tunic. Not even Higson's parents knew about the breastplate, and she had the overwhelming feeling that it should remain that way for their own safety. She carried her pack through the main room of the farmhouse and placed it just outside the front door. She quietly shut the door and turned back into the house.

Just as Carling entered the kitchen and began greeting Higson's family, the sound of pounding hooves approaching the cabin filled the room. This was followed by a knock on the front door of the quaint little cottage. Two Centaurs greeted Higson when he opened the door.

"Hello, Hero Higson," said Tibbals with a giggle, her arms opened wide, her eyes sparkling. "My brother, Tandum, and I have been sent by the leaders of our herd to help you."

"Find the stone?" answered Higson with surprise.

"Well, they didn't exactly tell us what you needed," Tibbals answered, "just that we are to help you. So if you need to find some sort of stone, we'll help you do that."

Higson's parents looked back and forth at their visitors and one another but said nothing. They seemed to know, by their silence, that things were changing and Higson and Carling were to be a part of it. Discreetly, they stepped out of the room.

At that moment, Carling brushed past Higson. "Tibbals! I'm so excited to see you again."

Tibbals reached down and wrapped her arms around Carling. "Oh, beautiful, wonderful Carling." She stood back up and introduced her brother.

Carling blinked, stunned by the handsome features of the Centaur colt standing before her. Tandum, unlike his palomino sister, was a glowing chestnut color, the hair of his head and his equine body the color of polished copper. His skin was darker than his sister's but radiated the same youthful glow. His chest, though covered with a pale blue shirt, was obviously well muscled, as was his entire body. Duende men and boys, though kind and thoughtful and a bit handsome in their own way, were nothing like this! Carling couldn't trust herself to speak.

"It is certainly a pleasure to meet you," Tandum said with a bow. "I regret missing the celebration that was held in your honor. But now, let's get to the purpose of our visit. My father and one of our herd elders, Adivino, have sent us to help you with some special assignment you've been given."

Carling forced herself to pull her eyes away from Tandum and look over at Tibbals. "You don't know what the assignment is?" she asked, remembering Vidente's admonition. The last thing she wanted was to put Tibbals in danger.

"Higson said something about finding a stone," said Tibbals.

Carling glanced over at Higson and raised her eyebrows. Her friend smiled sheepishly and shrugged his shoulders.

Tandum jumped in. "They didn't tell us, it is true, but it doesn't matter. After what you did for Tibbals and her friends, we will do anything for you."

A voice entered Carling's head, a voice belonging to the Wizard. *Show them.*

Carling opened her tunic, exposing the silver breastplate. Tibbals and Tandum gasped.

"That is so beautiful. Where did you get it?" asked Tibbals, awe in her voice.

"The Wizard of Crystonia gave it to me."

"Vidente?" asked Tandum. "You met the Wizard Vidente?"

Carling nodded.

"Could it be? I've heard about a silver breastplate...." He paused and his eyes opened wide as realization dawned. He stared at Carling, his mouth falling open. "You?"

Carling nodded again. She could feel a deep blush spread over her face.

Tibbals looked back and forth between the two. "So, is someone going to fill me in? Or are you going to let me remain oblivious?"

"The bearer of the silver breastplate is the rightful ruler of the kingdom," Tandum said, without taking his eyes off Carling. "Our herd has been waiting for its appearance for over a hundred years."

Tibbals caught her breath. "Carling? You?" For a moment, she just stared at her new friend. "Forgive me for being so surprised but you're a...a...Duende!"

"Don't worry," Carling said, looking down. "You aren't nearly as surprised as I am."

"Wow. That makes this assignment much more interesting." The filly reached down and placed a hand on either side of Carling's face. Lifting it up she gave her a warm smile.

Carling stepped back. Pointing to one of the holes in the breastplate she said, "I am to find the Stone of Mercy to place in the breastplate."

"Were you told where to find it?" asked Tandum.

Higson stepped in. "Vidente said the eagle, Baskus, has been guarding the stone. Do you know where we can find him?"

Tibbals' eyes twinkled. "Let's go visit Adivino. He is the wisest of all Centaurs. If anyone knows where to find Baskus, he will."

Tibbals took hold of one of Carling's hands and pulled her out of the cottage. Carling grabbed her pack once they were out the door. The filly lifted Carling to her back as Tandum placed Higson on his. Carling noticed Higson's bow and quiver full of arrows attached to his pack and smiled to herself. She didn't need to remind Higson of anything. A feeling of gratitude for this lifelong friend surged through her.

The two Centaurs turned and cantered away from the little cottage. Just as she had done the first time she rode a Centaur, Carling looked back. She saw Higson's parents watching them, a look of concern on their faces. She raised one hand and waved to them. She was filled with the awareness that her life would never be the same. The knowledge was painful. Slowly, and with much regret, she turned and faced the future.

CHAPTER 13

Meeting Adivino

THE COMPANIONS ENTERED THE clearing that surrounded Adivino's picturesque cottage. Round windows adorned the exterior. Flowering vines growing up the sides and along the roof added bright splashes of color. A large door, big enough for a Centaur, stood ajar. Once her Centaur friends came to a stop, Carling heard birds trilling in the flowering trees that surrounded the glade.

The shimmering signs of spring did nothing to quell the storm clouds of emotion that were building inside Carling. Fear and doubt dominated but were mixed with a small amount of excitement and eagerness to test herself. She looked over at Higson, trying to read his expression. No Luck. Higson sat stoically upon Tandum's back, his unblinking eyes looking directly ahead. His mouth was set in a straight line, his jaw firm.

Just as the four approached the front of the cottage, a very old Centaur stepped out to greet them. He wore a broad smile on his heavily wrinkled face. His gray hair was unkempt, as though it hadn't met a comb in several days. The muscles on his once-strong equine body now sagged from disuse. But the twinkle in his eyes told Carling his mind was still sharp.

"Tibbals and Tandum, you've brought the famous Carling and Higson to meet me. I couldn't be more pleased," he said, running his ink-stained fingers through his wild hair in a futile attempt to make himself more presentable.

"Adivino," said Tandum, "you sent us to help Carling with an important assignment."

Adivino nodded, the smile still on his face. "I did indeed. Tell me what help you need from me, my dear Carling," he said as he stepped up beside Tibbals. The old Centaur looked directly into Carling's eyes.

Carling forced herself to return the gaze. "I have been sent by the Wizard Vidente to find the Stone of Mercy."

"Ah. The Stone of Mercy. A very valuable stone. Do you know the holder of that stone will become the possessor of a forgiving heart? Mercy is one of the qualities of a great and noble leader. He or she knows how to balance justice and mercy." Adivino scratched the stubble on his chin and switched his thinning, gray tail. He patted her knee. "Yes, Carling, there is a time and a place for both. Neither should negate the other. The leader who forgets to be merciful becomes a tyrant, and her subjects suffer immensely." He winked his right eye.

"I will remember that. Thank you," whispered Carling.

Tandum, always efficient and focused, stepped up. "Adivino, the Wizard Vidente told Carling the eagle Baskus has been guarding the stone."

Adivino clapped his hands. "So, that's where Vidente has hidden it! That clever old Wizard. I suppose I should have guessed. Baskus owes his life to Vidente, after all. But that's another story."

"Do you know where we can find him?" asked Higson.

"Not precisely. But I do know the eagle likes to build his nests in Manyon Canyon."

Tibbals gasped. "Manyon Canyon! That's on the far side of Crystonia. It will take us two days to get there."

"The shortest way is through the Forest of Rumors and across the Echoing Plains," advised Adivino.

Tibbals glanced at her brother. "Will this be okay with Father?"

Tandum brushed his sister's question aside with the wave of a hand. "Father told us to fulfill the assignment," he said. "And we will do whatever it takes to do so."

Carling looked from one Centaur to the other, her eyes wide with wonder. The thought of going to Manyon Canyon frightened her. Until this time, she had barely wandered outside the little village of Duenton. Her forays into the forest with Higson had been adventure enough. Then the day came when she was taken to visit the great Centaur city of Minsheen. She shook her head. That seemed like such a long time ago, and yet it had only been a few days. *What a difference in a life a few days can make,* she thought to herself.

Her thoughts returned to the present and she felt herself get tense. Here she was at a stranger's cottage, being told she needed to travel a great distance through strange lands. She had heard many stories about the Forest of Rumors and Manyon Canyon, none of them good. She had been told of frightening creatures who inhabited the forest, a forest that was always dark. She had also heard stories of creatures who had entered Manyon Canyon and never returned...or did return, and were forever changed. Now they were to go to these foreboding places. She cocked her head and wondered why her companions' only concern seemed to be the distance. Perhaps those were just silly stories, she told herself.

CHAPTER 14

The Forest of Rumors

THE SUN WAS STILL new to the day when the adventurers set off for the Forest of Rumors. No one knew exactly how the forest had received its name...only a bunch of rumors surrounded it. But only Tandum had been to the densely wooded area before. That was with his father on group hunting expeditions. At that time, he had felt safe and protected by the stallions around him.

The Forest of Rumors was the stuff of childhood nightmares: ancient trees that tore at your face and clothing, thick undergrowth that tried to pull you down, and unidentifiable sounds that came from all directions at once. As Carling approached it with the others, she was sure her friends felt the same amount of trepidation she did, but no one said anything.

The beautiful, warm day disappeared the minute they entered the forest and were swallowed up by the thick canopy overhead and the ferns and vines that covered the ground. The entire forest smelled wet and musty, the air thick with humidity. At times, the forest would be silent, except for the sucking sounds as Tibbals and Tandum struggled to pull their hooves free of the mud. At other times, there would be sounds all around that caused the travelers to jump first one way, then the other. Carling took several deep breaths to try to calm her pounding heart. She wiped her forehead with the sleeve of her tunic.

Moving through the forest was difficult, even for the tall, strong Centaurs. They did their best to find a path between the trees, although there usually wasn't one. Often their chosen route would be blocked by tangles of rotting logs. Their strong hind legs lifted them up and over some barriers, but this often caused them to land in thick bogs of mud that tried to swallow them the moment their hooves touched down on the other side. They pushed and pulled with all their strength to keep their feet moving forward. Carling felt sorry for Tibbals as she struggled and she could see sweat forming on the filly's chest and flanks. The young Duende did her best to push low-hanging branches and dangling vines out of their way, but didn't think she was helping much.

After several hours of moving slowly through the dense, dark forest, Tandum came to a halt. "I think we need to rest for the night. The sun is getting low and, as little light as it offers in this Godforsaken place, we don't have a chance of getting through this forest in the dark. I know of a cabin Father and I used on our hunting trips. I don't think it is far away. I will lead you there."

No one argued.

Within about half an hour, and just as the sun's rays attempted to slide sideways through the trees, Tandum halted and raised his hand to both stop and silence the others. He cocked his head, then placed a finger to his lips. Quietly he tiptoed, as much as a Centaur is able on their hooves, a few feet farther. He reached out his arms and parted the brush in front of him and Higson. Carling and Tibbals stepped up beside them. It was then that they could hear the ruckus.

Loud laughter and talking were coming from the cabin that stood in the middle of the clearing ahead. The front door was ajar, and smoke was billowing from the stone chimney. As they watched, a group of Centaurs stumbled out the front door, laughing and joking with one another.

Carling gasped as she felt Tibbals become tense beneath her. These were the very same Centaurs who had attempted the kidnapping and attacked the village of Duenton a few days ago. They were easy to recognize. Their hair hung down to their shoulders in dirty curling locks. Their faces were covered with smudges of dirt, and scraggly beards dropped like strings of moss from their chins. Their strong upper bodies were covered in black leather vests, decorated with chains. Some wore bandages of torn cloth over the wounds inflicted upon them by Carling and Higson. These were members of the Heilodius herd that had split off from the Minsheen Centaurs.

It was easy to hear what the Centaurs were saying as they shouted back and forth to one another. Suddenly, what Carling heard made her heart stop.

"Did you see how that little Duende woman begged for her life?" said one large Heilodius Centaur. "Oh, please don't kill me. Please!" he mocked. The rest of the group that had now spilled out of the cabin and into the clearing responded with raucous laughter.

"Like you cared about her little life!" responded one. More laughter filled the glen.

"Ha, ha, Clank!" added another. "You are positively evil!"

The Centaur named Clank, the apparent leader of the group, raised his head high, clearly amused. "Yes, I am. Isn't it delightful!"

"At least her husband took it like a man!" choked out another between hiccups.

Carling couldn't take it anymore. She reached over her shoulder and removed an arrow from her quiver. Then she nocked the arrow on her bow, setting it over Tibbals' shoulder, and drew back, aiming for the heart of the Centaur named Clank.

Higson reached over and grabbed her arm, stopping her just before she released the arrow. "Carling," he whispered. "Stop!"

Keeping her eyes on her target, she hissed back, "He killed my parents. He needs to pay," and pulled her arm back an inch farther.

Tandum reached over and clasped her arrow. "Not yet, Carling. We don't want them to know we are here."

"If they come after us in the darkness, they might very well catch us. Then we would not get the Stone of Mercy," added Tibbals.

"But one of them would be dead," said Carling through clenched teeth.

"Yes, but you wouldn't complete your quest to get the stone. Right now, that is more important," said Higson, calmly but firmly.

"Right now I don't even care about the stone. I just want revenge. You heard him! He killed my parents! And they're laughing about it!"

"I understand why you're so angry. I would be, too," said Tibbals.

"But we must keep our eyes on the bigger goal," added Tandum.

"We must find the stone," said Higson.

Carling pursed her lips and lowered her bow and arrow.

Higson, Tibbals, and Tandum let out a collective sigh of relief. Then Higson reached over and put an arm around Carling's shoulders. "We can come back after we find the stone. If they're still here, you can do what you need to do."

Carling lowered her head and let the tears flow.

CHAPTER 15

The Echoing Plains

THE TWO CENTAURS AND their riders backed up silently and moved around the clearing, tying to ignore the boisterous laughter and shouting still audible through the trees. Once they reached the other side of the glen, they carried on through the darkness, guided only by Tandum's keen sense of direction, to where the Forest of Rumors met the Echoing Plains. From the edge of the forest, the plains spread out through the night, lit by the silver moon. The rolling hills looked like ocean waves, and the gentle breeze rustling the grasses sounded like whispered secrets. The soft scents of sage, blue gamma, and buffalo grass floated through the air.

"Let's rest here for the night," said Tandum.

Carling and Higson dropped to the ground. They pulled some rolls and cheese out of their bags. Together, the four adventurers curled up on the moss-covered ground and ate until they were filled. As they ate, no one said much of anything, each lost in their own thoughts and concerns. Carling and Higson rested against the shoulders of the two Centaurs.

Finally, Tandum broke the silence. "I will take the first watch," he whispered.

"Do you think we are in danger?" asked Higson.

Tibbals looked over at the little Duende and smiled kindly. "There are many rumors surrounding this forest. That's why it has its name. The Centaurs are not the only ones who hunt here. My father told me stories about hiding from a hunting party of Cyclops. It is possible that the Ogres travel through here as well. We wouldn't want to be caught unaware."

"I believe we must keep our quest a secret from the other races," Tandum added, "as well as from the Heilodius herd. They seek to rule the kingdom. If they knew a queen had been called, they would do anything in their power to stop her from qualifying."

"Tell me about the Heilodius herd," Carling said. "All I know is they were once part of your herd. What happened?"

Tibbals shook her head. "It is such a sad story. I can't bear to tell it," she said as she sniffed and wiped her moist eyes.

"I will," responded Tandum. "It all happened nearly fifty years ago, before Tibbals and I were even born. Our father was just elected to the leadership of the herd. At the time, a Cyclops named Zeriboum was attempting to hold the throne on Mount Heilodius and rule Crystonia. My father sent him an epistle saying the Minsheen herd did not recognize his authority and would not obey any of the edicts he was trying to impose upon the Centaurs. Father felt that simply living peacefully in the City of Minsheen would be enough. However, there were others of the ruling council of our herd who wanted to go to war with the Cyclops and take over the rule of Crystonia. Father felt that would make us no better than the Cyclops and refused to do it. As it turned out, the Ogres soon went to battle with the Cyclops, and Zeriboum was killed right on the throne, his blood pooling around the dais."

"Oh, Tandum," Tibbals exclaimed, "you don't have to give us all the gruesome details!"

"Well, I want them to know this is serious business."

"I think we get the idea," said Carling. "Please continue."

"As I was saying, Father wanted to live in peace and let the other races do the same. With the murder of Zeriboum, the throne of Crystonia was empty once again. That was enough temptation for several of the Minsheen herd's leadership. Three of them revolted against Father and the other council members. A great battle within the very council chambers broke out. First it was just a battle of words and ideas, but then swords were drawn. Several council members who were loyal to Father were killed, and Father himself was badly injured. When the battle was over, the dissidents were cast off the council. Not content to just agree to disagree, they gathered as many supporters as they could and left the City of Minsheen. That was the beginning of the Heilodius herd, named after the object of their ambition, the seat of power on Mount Heilodius." Tandum quit speaking and gazed off across the moonlit plains.

Carling had more questions, but she wasn't sure if now was the time to ask them. Tandum solved her quandary. He turned and looked down at her. "Do you have any more questions?"

"Actually, yes...if you feel like answering them."

"Please ask. As the future queen of Crystonia, you need to understand all the dynamics and intrigue going on in the kingdom."

"You said the Heilodius herd formed approximately fifty years ago."

Tandum nodded.

"How large a group is it now?"

"We don't know for sure. They began with the original dissenters and a couple dozen recruits from our herd. Very few mares and fillies went with them." He paused and looked over at Tibbals before continuing. "Some think the reason they tried to kidnap Tibbals and her friends is because they need more mares to increase the size of their herd."

Carling looked over at Tibbals and saw her friend draw back with revulsion.

"You see, Carling," Tandum continued, "very few of the Minsheen herd have joined their ranks in the intervening decades. A few of our herd, including my uncle, have disappeared. When that happens, we can only assume the missing have joined forces with the Heilodius or been the victim of some terrible accident. We don't know which would be worse," he added with a snort.

"I think we had best call it a night," said Tibbals. "I, for one, am totally exhausted.

Carling nodded. "Thank you for that information, Tandum," she said. "I am sure it will be very helpful." She snuggled in beside Tibbals and was soon fast asleep.

Higson, who had been listening intently, looked at Carling. Even in the darkness, she was beautiful. She looked so peaceful sleeping. Higson let out a long sigh and settled in to get some rest as well.

Carling woke with a start, escaping from a dream that caused her heart to pound and perspiration to bead up on her forehead. In her dream, the evil Centaur named Clank was standing over her mother. Her mother lay on the floor, her hands raised in a futile attempt to defend herself. Carling could feel her terror and see it in her eyes, which were wide with dread.

"Are you okay?" asked Tibbals, sensing Carling's tension.

"I just had a terrible dream."

Tibbals nodded. "I'm sorry. You have been through a lot. I can understand why it would present itself in bad dreams."

Higson and Tandum groaned and stretched. "Good morning," they said in unison.

"Good morning, sleepy heads," said Tibbals cheerfully.

Carling smiled in acknowledgment. The little Duende looked around her. The Echoing Plains looked much different in the morning sunlight. Gone were the silver waves, having been replaced by green rolling hills that looked as soft as pillows. Meadowlarks and mourning doves flitted from brush to tree and the tall grasses waved a greeting. The sun felt warm and welcoming on her face. The air smelled fresh and clean, a mixture of the forest behind them and the grasslands before them. Under ordinary circumstances, she would welcome the day with joy and excitement. But she had a feeling her life would never be ordinary again, and that saddened her. She took a deep breath and pushed herself up to stand, stiff from sleeping on the hard ground. Trying not to think too much, she pulled some fruit and rolls out of her pack and passed them around. Everyone ate enthusiastically, except her. She just couldn't shake the images from her dream.

Higson, seeing her downcast expression said, "What's the matter, Carling?"

She shook her head. "Nothing...Everything...Let's just get going and find this stone." The ever-present questions nagged at her again. Why me? Why was I selected to become the queen? Why did the Wizard send me on this quest?

Carling and Higson climbed up on the Centaurs' backs and wrapped their arms around Tibbals' and Tandum's waists. As the Centaurs began to carry them, it became clear that the Duende were both getting quite good at riding, and were now able to keep their bodies moving with the Centaurs. As the large creatures pushed their strong haunches from behind and stretched their long front legs forward, the rhythm of the movement was comforting to Carling. Before long, she realized she was smiling.

She glanced over at Higson and was pleased to see that he, too, was smiling.

They were heading toward the southwest, the sun sending their shadows to their sides. Carling looked up at the expansive blue sky. Never before had she been in a wide open space such as this. Her little village was surrounded by the forest. In a way, the closeness of the trees had always felt protective. Out here, she felt exposed; though to what, she couldn't say.

When the Centaurs reached a little pond surrounded by tall cattails, they stopped to fill their water flasks and take a rest. Carling leaped off Tibbals and pushed her way through the cattails. The plants rustled in complaint and sent white puffs of seed pods flying into the air. Carling dipped her hands in the cool water and brought them up to her face, letting the water refresh her as it ran down her cheeks. She closed her eyes and breathed in the warm prairie air.

Suddenly, she opened her violet eyes. In the distance she could hear a pounding sound. She had no idea what it could be. She turned and struggled back through the cattails to where Higson and the Centaurs were resting.

"Do you hear that sound?" she asked.

They stopped talking and listened. Higson even put his hand to his large, pointed ears. "Yes. I do hear something," he said.

"What do you suppose it is?" Carling asked.

"It's hard to say," responded Tandum. "This is called the Echoing Plains because of the strange and sometimes sinister sounds that float on the prairie winds. Sometimes they are simply magnifications of nothing at all. Other times, the sounds are bounced around so much that they become unrecognizable. And it's always hard to determine what direction the sound is coming from. We will carry on toward Manyon Canyon, but we'd be wise to keep our eyes open."

Tibbals stepped up to Carling. "Don't worry, little Carling," the filly said. "We will take care of you."

"Let's get going," Tandum said. "I want to reach the Canyon before the sun sets."

The band of travelers started out once again, making their own path. They traveled over rolling hills and across little ravines that had been cut into the sandy soil by the flash floods that always seem to arrive in summer and leave their mark for the rest of the year. There were few trees to provide shade, only a lonesome cottonwood now and again, sucking water from any tiny stream or pond it could find.

As they moved forward, Carling kept her pointed ears perked as she listened for the pounding sound. It seemed to her that it was getting louder, but, as Tandum had warned, it was impossible to tell from which direction it was coming. For all she knew, they were moving right toward it. At one particularly loud boom, she jerked in surprise, squeezing her legs tightly around Tibbals.

"I heard that, too, Carling. I can't tell what it was nor where it came from," Tibbals said in response to her rider's reaction.

Within minutes, they found out.

The Centaurs had just crested the tip of a grassy ridge when both Tandum and Tibbals stopped abruptly, lowered themselves to their knees, and ducked their heads. "Get off, Higson and Carling," commanded Tandum, "and get down flat on the ground."

"What is it?" asked Higson.

"Just do it!" said Tandum, rather harshly.

Carling was surprised by Tandum's response, but she and Higson instantly did as they were told.

Crouching on bent knees and hocks, Tandum and Tibbals crawled up the hillock until they could just peek over the top. Carling and Higson followed until they had scooted up beside the Centaurs.

Soon, four sets of eyes, one of which was violet, were taking in a frightening sight. On the other side of the mound upon which they were crouching was a wide gulley. And in the gulley was a large band of Cyclops.

Carling gasped and her hand flew to her mouth. Her face turned ashen and her chin began to tremble as fear flowed through her body. Her blood felt as though it had turned to ice. She had never seen such terrifying creatures. They were monsters by any sense of the word. Each one of them must have been ten feet tall at the least. Their upper bodies were muscular, the muscles in their arms and chests bulging. Their only clothing was a loin cloth made of animal skin that was tied around their waist. Their meager clothing was short enough to reveal legs covered with dense hair. Their feet were cloven hooves. A single thick horn that protruded straight up from the center of their skulls was surrounded by long, stringy hair. But the most frightening part was their faces. The Cyclops had large, protruding jaws and sharp teeth barely covered by black, blistered lips. They had only one eye which was located right in the middle of their forehead.

"Cyclops," whispered Tandum. The others nodded, not really needing to be told the obvious.

The Cyclops had built a fire as a make-shift forge. Some were using bellows to bring the fire to a higher temperature. Several of them inserted pieces of metal into the flames, drawing the metal out only when it glowed as orange as a sunset. Using large hammers, they pounded the metal into the shapes of swords and spears. Other members of the band could be seen grinding the edges of the swords to make them sharp. With the noise and the smoke, it was unlikely that they would have noticed the four observers.

Tandum slid backward down the hillside. The others followed.

"They're preparing for war," he said.

"Aren't they always?" responded Tibbals.

"Father said the Council had come to a truce with the Cyclops."

"So who are they preparing to fight?" asked Tibbals.

Tandum shook his head. "I don't know. Perhaps the Ogres...perhaps the Heilodius herd. When we return to Minsheen, we will need to report this to Father."

Carling glanced over at Higson. Her internal senses told her to flee. Instead, she reached over and grabbed his hand for security. He responded by giving her a weak smile and a squeeze of her hand.

The travelers left quickly, taking a course that gave them a wide berth around the gulley, enabling them to stay well away from the Cyclops. Aware that the Cyclops have a very keen sense of smell, it had to be a very wide berth.

The Centaurs began galloping to make up for lost time. They desperately wanted to reach Manyon Canyon before the sun set.

Just as the lowering sun was sending blue shadows over the prairie grass, the band of travelers stopped. Ahead of them, painted black by the shadows, a jagged scar cut across the Echoing Plains, slicing it in half. It zig-zagged its way northward toward the mountain range that bordered Mount Heilodius, the destined home of the ruler of Crystonia. Carling felt a shiver tickle her spine as she realized she was looking at the infamous Manyon Canyon. Now, more than ever, she hoped the stories she had heard were not true.

Tandum led them to the left and cantered down a gentle slope until they reached the mouth of the Canyon.

"I'm exhausted," whispered Tibbals.

Carling jumped off Tibbals and offered her a drink of water.

As her friend drank, Carling looked ahead into the canyon. A large and boisterous stream wove its way out of the deep gorge, bouncing against rocks and boulders. The high stone walls to either side were covered with steps and crags that had been formed by centuries of abuse from wind and water. The rough cliff walls reached up hundreds of feet. On many of the ledges, curling pine trees had managed to carve out a home for themselves. Birds, large and small, flitted from one tree to another, making loud squawking and chirping sounds as they did so. While marmots, rabbits, and coyotes scurried around the base of the cliffs, big horn sheep leapt from one rocky shelf to the next. The entire canyon seemed to be alive.

Half of the canyon was already in the dark from the shadows cast by the setting sun. Clearly, there was little daylight left.

"How will we find Baskus? It's so large," exclaimed Carling.

Tandum shook his head as he looked to the west. "We didn't make it in time. We will have to find a place to camp for another night and begin our search in the morning."

Carling's heart felt like it was shrinking. She pressed her lips tightly together. Her shoulders slumped as she heaved a heavy sigh.

Higson came to her side. "It's okay, Carling," he said, patting her gently on the shoulder. "We'll find the great eagle tomorrow."

Carling felt her body relax as she looked up into Higson's kind eyes. "You're right, Higson. We'll find him tomorrow."

CHAPTER 16

In the Fog

NO SUN KISSED HER cheek. No birds sang a welcome to the new day. Carling awoke to find herself surrounded by a dense fog that covered the ground and filled the canyon. Everything was cold and silent. She could barely see beyond a few feet. Her heart sank. *How will we ever find Baskus in this?* she asked herself.

Of immediate concern was the fact she couldn't see any of her companions due to the thick fog. "Higson? Tibbals? Tandum? Is anyone there?" The silence sent her heart racing. "Where is everyone?" Carling felt perspiration beading on her forehead even in the cold as she strained to hear a response. She walked carefully around in circles, looking for any sign of her friends, trying not to panic. It didn't take her long to realize Higson, Tibbles, and Tandum and their packs of supplies were gone.

Carling tried to stay calm so she could think rationally. She rubbed her hands together to warm them while she considered possible explanations. Perhaps they had just ventured out to find water or firewood. Perhaps they were just scouting out the canyon in search of a trail to take. They would never leave her, she reasoned. They would be back for her. But no matter how hard Carling tried to make some sort of sense out of all of this, she could not shake the foreboding feeling that her friends were in danger.

After what seemed forever, the screech of a raptor broke the ominous silence. By the sound it made, Carling was sure it was a very large bird. A dark apparition appeared in the fog, getting larger as the sound of flapping wings grew louder. The shape became clearer the closer it got, and it was soon obvious that the creature coming toward her through the fog was large enough to be an eagle.

Carling stared at the bird as it approached and sent out occasional screeches. She wasn't sure if she should run and hide or stay where she was. She chose to stand firm and wait. Soon it was directly over her and circling around, calling out almost frantically now. Just as it flew down to within a few feet of her, one of the bird's large talons opened wide and a stunning green stone, circular in shape, fell to the ground at her feet. Carling bent to look at it. It was the most beautiful stone she had ever seen. The color was the green of the forest that she loved. The shape had not been sculpted by a human hand. It was too perfect. Even the skilled Duende artisans would not have been able to create such a stone. The stone was both beautiful and frightening, and she knew immediately that this was the Stone of Mercy that she was seeking. From what little Vidente had told her, she also knew this stone held great power, a power she did not understand. That frightened her.

Hesitantly, she reached out and picked it up, her hands shaking. Biting her lip, she looked up toward the bird. Surely this was the great eagle called Baskus. The raptor let out another loud cry, circled her, then started back in the direction from which it had come, its large head turning back to look at her.

Carling had the clear impression that she was to follow him. She pulled aside her cloak and, with trembling hands, placed the stone in the round hole cut into the left front of her silver breastplate. The stone fit perfectly and, as though alive, nestled into place. It seemed to know this was where it belonged. Instantly, a surge of energy flowed through Carling's veins like electricity. She gasped and fell backward onto the ground, her body tingling. Shivering uncontrollably, she pushed herself back up to her feet. Her heart was pounding rapidly and her thoughts were confused in a mixture of fear and amazement.

She stood in place for a moment, trying to get her bearings yet eager to follow Baskus. Without taking the time to consider what possessing the stone meant to her and the future of Crystonia, and still feeling a bit disoriented, Carling grabbed her pack and started running to catch up with the eagle. Her body felt indescribably strong, like it could run forever. She had never felt like this before.

Carling wondered how much Baskus understood about the magic the stone contained. According to the old Centaur, Adivino, the eagle had been guarding it for a long time.

The bird stayed low to the ground and just close enough for Carling to be able to see it despite the fog. She could see nothing on either side of her, so she kept her eyes on the dark shape of the bird and moved swiftly in order to stay with him.

Clusters of trees that bordered the river appeared out of nowhere and just as quickly disappeared. Enormous rocks loomed over her, looking like monsters in the mist. In the swirling vapor around her, Carling didn't see the edge of the rift that the elements had carved into the canyon floor. Before she could catch herself, she found herself tumbling down, bouncing and rolling the few feet to the sandy base. She quickly pushed herself to her knees, brushed off her clothing, and checked for damage. Her face tightened as she clenched her teeth and she frowned as she rubbed her sore shoulders and hips.

Carling scampered to her feet and looked around, frantically searching through the gray fog for the bird. She didn't have to search long. With a loud screech and a flap of its wings, the giant bird reappeared in front of her face. This time it was so close that Carling was able to get a good look at it. The raptor was an elegant golden eagle, much larger than any eagle she had ever seen. The feathers on its head and down its back were the color of polished brass. Its eyes were round and black as coal. Its wings had a span of several arm lengths.

The beautiful bird screeched again and started flying away, deeper into the canyon.

"Baskus. Wait, Baskus," Carling cried out.

By way of response, the giant bird screeched but kept flying.

Carling knitted her eyebrows and scowled, pressing her hands on her hips in irritation. Her knuckles moved against the unyielding metal of the silver breastplate. She took in and released a deep breath, then started forward again, realizing she had no alternative but to follow. Her only hope was that Baskus was there to help her find her companions.

After following Baskus for many minutes, Carling heard voices reverberating through the fog. "Let go of us. Let us go right now!" It was Tibbals. Carling recognized her voice immediately.

Baskus swooped back toward her. He tilted his wings, back-flapped to slow his descent, and landed on the ground in front of her. He immediately extended his wings wide to both sides, stopping her in her tracks.

"What is it, Baskus?" Carling asked, her voice low. "What's going on?"

The eagle turned his entire body toward the loud voices but kept his wings outstretched. Baskus moved forward slowly, walking like the elegant creature that he was, his head high, his body upright. Carling followed behind, not feeling nearly so elegant.

The voices and sounds of movement and struggling got louder. At first Carling could see only shifting shadows. Hearing Tibbals cry out and occasional grunts and growls from Tandum made her want to call to them, to tell them she was there. Her instincts and the eagle's behavior, however, told her to keep silent. She was sure one of the shapes was Higson, but she heard no sounds coming from him. She lifted her feet and set them back down silently, moving forward with the stealth of a cat. The cold, damp mist made her shiver and she wrapped her arms around her body, feeling the silver breastplate that covered her torso. It provided neither warmth nor comfort.

As she walked forward, a sudden warm breeze brushed past her face like a feather. She was surprised by the abrupt change in temperature, which took the coldness and dampness with it. Soon, the shapes moved into sharp focus, as though a lens had been adjusted to clarify the scene. Carling could now clearly see Tibbals, Tandum, and Higson. Tied up with ropes, they were being dragged by nearly a dozen Fauns. Tibbals held onto the ropes that were around her waist, struggling against them and complaining with each step. Tandum and Higson seemed more resigned, heads bowed, fists clenched at their sides, trudging along.

Carling knew that the Fauns had, several years ago, sold their souls to the Cyclops. The half-goat, half-human race agreed to be servants to the one-eyed monsters in exchange for protection. This alliance had surprised the rest of the races in Crystonia. The Duende were not alone in their perception that the Fauns were fun-loving creatures who enjoyed nothing more than to play their flutes and dance around the forest glens. But for the last dozen years or so, the Fauns were never encountered in the woods unless they were doing the bidding of their cruel masters.

Carling's violet eyes opened wide in amazement. Feelings of curiosity and anger battled for her attention. *Why are they taking them?* she asked herself. *Where are they taking them? And why didn't they take me?*

Baskus stopped and turned his head from side to side. He half hopped, half flew to the right, toward a jagged vertical crack in the canyon wall. Carling followed. With a toss of his head and beak, the giant bird motioned for Carling to step into the crack. It was shallow but just deep enough for her to fit inside. She turned and faced the bird. His round black eyes peered into hers and held her there for a moment. Then, with a powerful downward flap of his wings, Baskus lifted off the ground. Carling, her heart leaping to her throat, bolted out of the crevasse. She was immediately pushed back as Baskus circled and flew past her. With a loud screech, the bird ascended into the newly blue sky. Clutching the rough stones that surrounded her, Carling watched him go.

CHAPTER 17

The Fauns

CARLING WANTED TO CALL out to Baskus and plead with him to stay. But she bit her lip and tried to decide what to do. Baskus clearly wanted her to stay where he had put her.

Carling shifted her attention back to her friends as they continued to be pulled up the base of the canyon by the Fauns. Tibbals was still pulling at the ropes and complaining.

When the Fauns had pulled their captives a good distance away, Carling sucked in her breath and stepped out of the crack in the rock. She bent low and hurried forward, keeping herself close to the canyon wall. Not watching where she was placing her feet, her foot kicked a loose rock, sending it bouncing down a slippery rock slope. The sound was amplified by the canyon walls. One of the Fauns at the side of the group stopped and turned around. Carling dropped to the ground, making herself as small as possible. The young Duende closed her eyes in a futile attempt to become invisible. She held her breath and listened. Carling felt her hands get clammy. After several minutes, she dared to open her eyes, raise her head a little, and look ahead. The Fauns and their prisoners had continued to move forward. She saw no sign of the guard who had looked around.

Assuming the Faun who heard the rock had moved ahead with the rest, Carling stood up just enough to straighten her legs. Still bent over, she moved forward, more careful this time as to where she placed her feet.

Carling traveled only a short distance, hurrying as quickly as she dared in an effort to catch up with her friends, when she approached a yellow and red rock outcropping. The stones were dotted with little desert flowers. Suddenly, a Faun leaped out from behind it. Carling gasped, stopped, and jerked upright. She recognized the Faun as the guard who had turned around at the sound of the bouncing rock. She held her breath as she carefully examined him. She had never seen a Faun in real life; she had only heard about them from tales told in front of the fireplace on winter nights. This Faun was only a little taller than she was as it stood upright on two, strong, hairy, goat-like legs with cloven hooves. His upper body was like that of a human, but his head was much different. Two curling horns sprouted from the side of his head. Two floppy ears hung halfway to his shoulders. A shock of red hair, like a forelock, fell between his dark, round eyes. A bushy red beard covered his chin and jawline, and the brittle hair had been plaited into a braid that hung down from the center of his chin. A rope was wound across his chest. Bands of gold adorned his arms and wrists, and he held a spear in his hand, which he was now pointing at her.

Carling's breath caught in her throat and she stumbled backward, falling to the ground.

"Get out of here!" commanded the odd-looking beast.

Carling let out a loud breath and raised her chin in defiance. "I will not leave without my friends."

"Please, Missy. Get out of here!" the Faun repeated more forcefully.

Carling scrambled to her feet. With boldness that surprised even her, she replied, "I said 'no'. I will not leave. Why have you taken my friends and where are you going with them?"

"We're just followin' orders. Now leave." His face softened a little, his voice developing a gentler tone. "It isn't safe here."

"Why didn't you take me when you took them?" asked Carling.

The Faun's eyes lowered until they were looking at the silver breastplate, visible only slightly beneath her cloak. Carling wrapped her cloak more tightly around her body in an attempt to hide the armor.

"You're wearin' the silver breastplate. We was afraid to touch ya."

"What do you know about the silver breastplate?"

"We've heard stories."

"What stories?"

"The rightful heir to the throne of Crystonia will be clothed in a silver breastplate." The Faun paused and looked directly into her violet eyes. "Is that you?"

Carling didn't answer. Instead, she broke away from his gaze and looked beyond him to where her friends were disappearing into the distance. "I must save my friends. Please step out of my way."

"I can't let ya go. It would not be safe." He paused and looked toward his retreating comrades. He turned back and whispered, "You must understand I'm takin' a great risk to my own safety by tryin' to help you."

"Who is making you do this?"

"We do the Cyclops' bidding," he answered, his gaze lowered in apparent shame.

"Why do they want Tibbals, Tandum, and Higson?"

"I don't know the answer Missy. We just follow the orders we're given."

"Well, I won't let the Cyclops take them. I must stop them," she said. Raising her chin and setting her jaw, she stepped forward, pushing the spear aside. The Faun backed away, as though afraid to be too near her.

No longer concerned about remaining hidden, Carling began running.

"Missy, Missy. Please come back here," the Faun softly cried out to her as he ran to catch up. "It's not safe, like I told ya. Please stop!"

Carling felt irritation flow through her. Her mouth formed into a tight frown as she clenched her fists. But she didn't stop. Keeping her eyes focused on the departing figures of her friends, she pumped her arms and ran even more quickly.

"Missy, you don't understand. The Cyclops, them be terrible beasts. I fear what they might do to ya," the Faun cried, now at her side and easily keeping up stride for stride, pumping his arms and swinging his spear forward and back. He grabbed her arm with his free hand in an attempt to stop her.

"Let go of me," Carling cried without slowing down. The Duende jerked her arm away, causing red marks from the Faun's fingers to form on her skin.

The Faun continued to plead with her. "Please, Missy. Please, Missy," he said. "I don't want ya to get hurt."

"Then you shouldn't have taken my friends," Carling responded, still running directly toward Higson, Tibbals, Tandum, and the Fauns who were pulling them along.

"And what do ya think you're goin' to do when you get to 'em?" asked the Faun. "I can't help you and you're all alone."

Carling stopped and put her hands on her hips. She pressed her lips tightly together and knit her brows, breathing heavily from her run. The Faun stopped beside her.

"I don't know. I'll just have to figure it out as I go." She rubbed her temples, then looked directly at the Faun. "Why can't you help me?"

"'Cause, in case you haven't noticed before, I'm a Faun. I am supposed to be one of them," he said, pointing ahead at the retreating group.

"Then why are you here with me?"

The Faun sucked in a deep breath and let it out slowly. "'Cause I don't like what's goin' on. I don't like being enslaved to the Cyclops and I don't like harmin' innocent creatures."

Carling looked deeply into his eyes, trying to figure out if the stranger was being sincere or just trying to entrap her. As she studied his dark round eyes, she saw a sadness there coupled with genuine concern. It touched her heart and she reached out and took his hand. "You stay here," she said with a smile. "I will go alone." She let go of his hand, turned and started running again.

CHAPTER 18

Saving Her Friends

AS SHE RAN, CARLING tried to formulate a plan in her mind. The only weapon she had was her bow and a quiver full of arrows. Fortunately, she was quite good at using them. She looked from side to side at the canyon walls, searching for a place to climb up, hoping to get above and ahead of the Fauns. She was gradually catching up with the group due primarily to Tibbals' persistent resistance and Carling's own speed.

When Carling was just a short distance behind the band of Fauns and their captives, she still didn't have a plan. From her right, Carling heard something.

"Shhhh. Missy. Shhhh. Come over here."

Carling slowed her pace and turned her head. The Faun she had met was motioning for her to come over closer to the cliff. Feeling a tinge of irritation she thought, *What now?* Regardless, she jogged over. She put her hands on her hips and raised her eyebrows, waiting for an explanation.

"Follow me," the Faun whispered. "There's a stream up ahead. If we can get across it before the others, we can wait on the far side an' ambush 'em when they cross."

"I thought you wouldn't help me?"

The Faun grinned. "A fella has a right to change his mind, don't he?"

Carling smiled. She was pleased to have company, even if this Faun was, as yet, little more than a stranger. "Let's do this, then," she said.

They ran along the side of the cliff, trying to be as quiet as they could be. Tibbals was continuing to make a ruckus and being as difficult as possible. Her arms were tied behind her back, but she bucked and reared as she shrieked and complained. As concerned as she was, Carling couldn't help but smile as she observed her friend's tenacity in action.

The Fauns dragging Tibbals along weren't as impressed and were clearly getting irritated. "Come on, you stupid Centaur," growled one as he jerked on the ropes that were wrapped around the filly's neck. "We don't have all day, you know."

"Ouch! You're hurting me. This rope will probably leave ugly red marks on my neck. I want it off right now!"

The constant distraction created by Tibbals worked to Carling's advantage, enabling her and the Faun to get in front of the group without being noticed. Up ahead, the canyon wall split open in a large crag to the right. A wide stream flowed out of the mountains, carrying the frigid water from the melting snow packs that still glistened in the mountains to the north. Carling and her companion rounded the corner and hurried up the side of the stream until they found a fallen tree trunk that had been carried down the fast-flowing water and now lay wedged between two boulders. It formed a narrow and slippery, but adequate, bridge across the icy cold water.

Carling crossed first, her lithe body carrying her swiftly across to the other side. The Faun had a bit more trouble as his cloven hooves slipped first to one side then to the other. He finally gave up that attempt and, dropping to his hands and hocks, crawled across, gripping the bark with his long fingernails.

Once they were both on land again, they wove through the trees and brush that were feeding off the fresh water and growing thick and lush on the north side of the bouncing stream. A small doe pounced out of a thicket, causing Carling to gasp and stop midstride. The Faun, not seeing Carling stop, ran into her from behind. She fell forward, landing in a brittle scrub oak, and cried out in both shock and pain but quickly covered her mouth to muffle her cry.

The Faun stepped up to her and extended his hands.

Giving him her best frown, she cocked her head and knit her brows. She wanted him to know she was not pleased to be sitting in a scratchy bush.

"Oh, Missy," the Faun whispered. "I'm so sorry. Twas an accident it twas. I promise. I'll be more careful. Let me help you up."

Carling opened her mouth to say something, then thought better of it. Instead, she clamped her mouth shut and reached out to take his hands. With amazing ease, he pulled her to her feet and started to brush the leaves and sticks off her cloak.

She pushed his hands away. "We don't have time. They'll be crossing the river soon. We need to get moving."

They ran through the trees, whose leaves cast lacy shadows on the ground. When they reached the river's edge at the point where they anticipated the captors would cross, Carling climbed into a bent pine tree, settled herself on a branch, nocked an arrow, and waited.

The Faun had an idea of his own. Removing the rope from across his chest, he tied one end to the tree that now concealed Carling and dashed to the west as far as the rope would stretch. He lowered the rope to the ground and waited, intending to trip the other Fauns when they arrived.

Their patience was soon rewarded.

Bursting out of the trees that lined the stream, the first of the Fauns aggressively approached the fast-flowing water. They didn't hesitate as they bound into the river. Their strong, hairy legs pushed through the powerful current, their cloven hooves slipping on the slimy rocks. But they continued to move forward.

Carling tightened her grip on her bow, held her breath, and took aim at the Faun in front. Before she could release her arrow, though, something dropped from the sky, hitting her intended target squarely on the head. He collapsed in the water, and a narrow ribbon of red immediately began flowing downstream from where he lay.

More dark objects fell. Mass confusion erupted as the Fauns in the water scrambled to get to safety...without having any idea where safety might be.

Carling looked up, and then her mouth fell open and her eyes bulged. She could not believe what she was seeing. Overhead, a dozen or more eagles were circling, each clasping a large rock. One by one, they were dropping the sharp, heavy stones onto the Fauns with surprising accuracy.

Below the gnarled pine tree in which Carling sat, her new partner was bouncing up and down and cheering. She watched him and smiled, realizing for the first time that she didn't even know his name.

On the far side of the river, Tibbals, Tandum, and Higson escaped from the Fauns by helping each other untie the ropes that held them bound. As injured Fauns climbed out of the stream, the Centaurs and the Duende rushed forward and tied them up in their own ropes. As the eagles flew away, their task complete, Carling cheered and called out to her friends. When they looked in her direction, surprise registered clearly on their faces as they realized it was Carling sitting in a tree, waving at them.

Suddenly, Carling felt a burning in her chest. Her hand flew to the breastplate and covered the green stone that was newly mounted in its place. She knew there was something she must do. But what? She looked back down at the rushing stream. The first Faun that had been felled by the eagles was still in the water, wedged between two boulders. Blood was still flowing downstream from the gash in his head. He wasn't moving.

Carling swung down from the branch on which she was sitting and dropped to the ground. She ran to the bank of the stream and got as close as she could to the injured Faun. She pulled her quiver and bow off her shoulder and unhooked her cloak, dropping all to the ground. The silver breastplate sparkled in the sun, sending out rays of light that caught the attention of all around, most of whom had struggled back to the far shore. Everyone, including Higson, Tibbals, and Tandum, stopped what they were doing and watched.

Carling stepped into the stream. The icy cold water made her suck in her breath and pause for just a moment. She gritted her teeth and stepped forward, placing her feet carefully on the rocks. One foot at a time, she moved into the rushing water, holding her arms out in an attempt to balance herself. Her teeth started chattering and she could feel her feet and legs getting numb but she carried on, keeping her eyes on the injured Faun.

"Carling, go back," shouted Tandum from across the stream. "Let him die."

Carling didn't look up. Didn't acknowledge. She just kept stepping from one rock to the next, trying desperately to keep her balance.

The young Duende had nearly reached her target when her foot stepped onto a rock that rolled out from under her the minute she put her weight on it. Down she went into the frigid water. The water bounced over her as though she were just one more rock to overcome. She pushed herself up, choking and gasping for air. After wiping her wet hair out of her eyes, she pulled herself through the water on her hands and knees.

With tremendous effort, Carling reached the injured Faun. "I'm here to help you," she shouted above the rushing water.

There was no response.

Carling pressed her ear against his chest. She could hear a soft but slow heartbeat and felt his chest move up and down ever so slightly. He was alive, but unconscious. Grasping his arms, she started pulling. She was able to get his body out from between the boulders, but as soon as she got him into the current, the force of the water began pushing him downstream again. Trying to cut across the stream was more difficult than she ever could have imagined it would be, had she taken the time to think about it...which she hadn't. She'd just reacted to the feeling within that told her to save the Faun.

Slipping on the rocks and trying to keep the Faun afloat was proving to be more exhausting than her body could manage. Just when she thought it was hopeless, however, Carling was bumped from behind.

"I'll help you." It was Higson. Soaking wet, and not extremely pleased based upon the look on his face, he remained Carling's loyal friend, just the same. Together, the two Duende managed to get the limp body to the shore.

"Now," said Higson, his hands on his knees as he gasped for breath. "Do you want to tell me why we did that?"

"He's a fellow Crystonian."

Higson looked at her askance. "Yeah, and he tried to capture us. So why are we saving him?"

Carling reached over and hugged Higson. "I don't really know, except that we must."

"Okay," he said with a snort. "You're the boss."

"Let's get to work healing his injuries," Carly suggested.

"Do you need this?"

Carling looked around. The Faun that had helped her was standing there with her bag. Higson jerked backward, holding his hands up in defense of an anticipated attack.

"Don't worry, Higson. This is my friend." Turning back to the Faun she said, "I don't even know your name."

Setting the bag down and extending his hand, he said with a smile and a twinkle in his eye, "I'm Pikins, but you kin call me Pik."

Carling shook his hand. "Well, Pik, thanks ever so much for helping me. Now let's get these Fauns doctored up."

Soaking wet and shivering, Carling grabbed her cloak from her bag and covered the Faun she and Higson had pulled from the water. She took a piece of clothing from her bag and ripped it in shreds. As she looked down at the deep gash on the Faun's head, she felt her stomach turn and bile sting her throat. Blood was not something she enjoyed seeing. Pressing her lips together, she set to work. She used some of the strips of fabric to apply enough pressure to stop the bleeding. She used others to wrap around his head, weaving them over and under his horns so they would be secure. As she did so, the Faun's eyes opened and he reached up and grabbed one of her wrists. "What happened?" he said.

"You're the victim of an attack by eagles," she said with a warm smile.

The Faun raised his eyebrows and his mouth dropped open as he gazed into her violet eyes. "Eagles?"

Carling nodded. "I guess they didn't like you capturing my friends."

The Faun looked away. "Why did you save me?" he said in a whisper.

Carling patted his shoulder. "What you did was wrong, but you don't deserve to die."

He looked back at her, his face ashen, his lips trembling. "It would have been better for me to die in the river. The Cyclops will not be pleased that we failed in our assignment. They have terrible tempers. They will punish all of us, perhaps to our deaths."

Carling became aware of four hooves standing beside them. She looked up into Tandum's face. It was not a happy expression that he wore. His lips were pressed together, his eyes narrowed. His arms were crossed tightly across his chest. "He's right, you know. You should have left him to die."

Carling stood, her voice soft. "We can't do that, Tandum. We need to treat others with mercy."

Tandum looked down at her sparkling silver breastplate. "You have the stone...the Stone of Mercy. So that's what this is all about. Now we have to show mercy to even our enemies?"

"Yes. Even our enemies."

Tandum snorted. "We'll see about that."

Tibbals trotted up beside her brother. "Carling! You have the stone. It's so beautiful. Look how it sparkles! How did you get it?" she said, excitement making her voice high pitched as her words tumbled out on top of one another.

Her enthusiasm made Carling smile. She related the story of the appearance of Baskus in the fog and his leading her to find them. "I have no doubt that Baskus arranged the aerial attack that saved you," she added.

Tandum blew out a loud breath. "Well, I'm glad you got the stone so we can turn around and get out of this awful canyon. But what are we going to do with all of these Fauns?"

"Can't we just let them go?" asked Higson.

"Oh, please take us with you," pleaded Pik. "We have no place else to go!"

The injured Faun still sitting on the ground joined in. "Yes, if we go back to the Cyclops, they will either torture us or kill us...or both," he said with a shudder.

The Centaurs and Duende looked back and forth at one another. Carling looked into each of their faces, unable to read what her friends were thinking.

Tandum spoke first. "We can't possibly take them with us. They will slow us down too much. We have a three-day journey for just the four of us. They can't keep up."

Tibbals looked up at her big brother. "I know you are angry with them for trying to capture us. I understand that, of course. But we can't be responsible for their execution."

"Maybe they should have thought of that before they signed up to help the Cyclops," Tandum replied, his voice rising.

Higson spoke up. "Tandum, I understand why you are angry and you have every right to be. If truth be told, I'm angry, too. They were willing to turn us over to the Cyclops. Who knows what would have happened to us? However, I don't want their lives on my conscience. Isn't there something we can do to help them?"

Tandum snorted and turned his magnificent body around, swishing his tail as he did so.

Carling felt her heart ache. The last thing she wanted was to create a rift between her friends.

When Tandum turned back around, however, the expression on his face had softened. He wasn't quite smiling, but he wasn't frowning, either. Looking directly at Carling, he said, "The choice is yours and I will abide by whatever you decide."

Carling felt tears stinging her eyes. She smiled up at this Centaur whom she already loved so much. She turned back and looked down at the injured Faun, then over at Pik. "It is true that you can't possibly keep up with Tibbals and Tandum," she said, chuckling before adding, "I couldn't, either, if they didn't carry me along. We also did not bring enough food and supplies to last us even the three days we have left to travel." She sighed. "Therefore, I would like to make a proposal."

Pik's eyes opened wide and the Faun leaned forward a little, appearing hopeful that he would hear good news.

"Pik," Carling said, "do you think you could get your group together and bring them to Duenton? It will take you several days and you will have to be careful not to be discovered. But when you arrive, we will have a place for you in our village."

CHAPTER 19

Leaving the Canyon

PIK RAN TO CARLING and threw his arms around her. He picked her up and swung her around so quickly that her legs flew out behind her. Carling released her tension with a giggle. "Pik, put me down, you silly beast!"

He lowered her gently to the ground, his face red. "I'm sorry. I don't know what got in ta me. It's just that this is the most wonderful offer I have ever heard." Then he paused and put one finger to the side of his bushy beard. "What will your villagers say?"

Carling really hadn't thought that far. "I don't know, but let *us* worry about that. You just get your Fauns to our village."

Carling and Higson mounted their Centaurs and bid the Fauns farewell. The Centaurs left the canyon by cantering toward the spot where they had entered the evening before. It didn't take them long to get to the mouth of Manyon Canyon and turn onto the Echoing Plains.

The sun beat on their backs as the warm air blew hair and tails aloft. Meadowlarks and mourning doves sang out a greeting. Carling noticed none of this, however. As her body moved in rhythm with her friend's rocking gallop. Her mind was busy reviewing all that had just occurred. In many ways, she felt amazed by her own behavior. In other ways, what she'd just done scared her. She knew the stone she wore on her chest had caused her to behave in a dangerous manner, all in the name of mercy. Life was never going to be the same for her, she knew that for a fact. She felt like she was stepping into the darkness and hoped there would be a light to guide her.

The Echoing Plains still carried the ominous sounds of the Cyclops across the rolling hills as the monsters forged and hammered their weapons. They were preparing for war. A shiver tickled Carling's spine. She knew she would have to be involved. Not only that, but she would have to see it through to the end when someone would finally hold the ruling throne atop Mount Heilodious. She would not have chosen this life.

As her thoughts went to her mother, Carling felt tears sting the backs of her eyes. Her throat constricted in sorrow. In an instant, a new realization dawned and she knew her mother had understood what the silver breastplate would mean for Carling. Her mother had hidden it from her, not even mentioning it until she was dying. Clearly, she had wanted to protect Carling. Now she was gone and Carling was on her own...on her own except for her friends. Carling reached around Tibbals' waist and pressed her cheek against the filly's shoulder, letting her tears wet the Centaur's billowing blouse. Tibbals reached

back with one of her hands and gently caressed the Duende, even as she kept carrying her toward the future.

CHAPTER 20

A Night in the Forest

TANDUM AND TIBBALS KEPT moving long into the night, winding over hills and through gullies as they crossed the Echoing Plains by the light of the full moon. At long last, they entered the darkness of the Forest of Rumors. Carling had fallen asleep, soothed by the rocking motion of her Centaur friend's smooth gait. She awoke when Tibbals slowed to a much-deserved walk. Carling instantly became alert as she looked around at the looming trees and the ominous shadows that surrounded them.

"We're in the Forest of Rumors! How did you cross the Plains so quickly?"

Tibbals stopped and stretched. With a weary voice she said, "It didn't feel like it went quickly to me!"

Immediately shamed by her insensitivity, Carling leaped off her friend's back. "I'm so sorry, Tibbals. You must be exhausted. What can I do for you?"

"Just let me sleep," Tibbals said with a weak smile. Looking down at her hooves whose sparkling polish was now chipped and dulled she added, "And some new hoof polish wouldn't hurt either."

Carling smiled. "I wish I had some for you," she said sincerely.

Tandum and Higson moved ahead, searching for a safe place to rest for the remainder of the night. They returned shortly and led Carling and Tibbals to a well-protected, though tiny, glen. Carling walked alongside Tibbals, rubbing her sore, sweat-covered body as they followed Tandum and Higson to the little clearing.

What the boys found was the perfect hideaway in which to bed down for the night. It was accessed by crawling under a bent-over tree, the branches of which formed a pine-needle curtain. Once in the circular clearing, the members of the little group were protected by a thick wall of brush and a canopy of branches and leaves. For the first time since leaving Higson's home, Carling felt safe.

Tibbals and Tandum collapsed and instantly fell asleep, Tandum snoring contentedly, Tibbals humming in her sleep.

Higson took Carling's hand and led her to one side of the glen, where they sat down beside each other. "Carling," Higson began, his dark eyes peering into his friend's violet eyes, "how are you feeling?"

"Frightened," she responded.

"I would be, too. The very thought of becoming the queen of Crystonia must be a heavy burden. I'd probably want to run away." Higson said this with a smile, but concern shone in his eyes.

Carling bit her lip. "I do feel like that," she finally said. "I am not qualified to lead anyone, let alone a country. I feel so alone..." As her voice trailed off, she gazed up toward the branches that intertwined above their heads.

Higson gave her hand a squeeze. "Oh, but you will never be alone," he said. "Tibbals and I have already promised each other that we will stay by your side. I'm sure Tandum will, too. And now you have many new friends in the Fauns. Speaking of the Fauns, have I told you what a remarkable thing you did back there? Of course, I must admit, I did think you were a little crazy!"

"It wasn't me. It was the Stone of Mercy." Carling pivoted her body so she was staring straight at Higson. "From the moment I put the stone in the breastplate, I felt a most remarkable power. It's impossible to explain. But I know that what I said and did was because of the stone."

Higson nodded. "I believe you. If the stones didn't hold power, the Wizard would not be sending you to gather them." He ran his fingers through his thick, brown hair. "We still have three more to find."

"Yes," Carling said. "That's scary, too. The Wizard said there would be those who would try to stop us. Oh, Higson," she added with a forlorn sigh, her body starting to tremble at the thought of what they'd just endured...and what lay ahead.

Higson wrapped his arms around her. "Whatever happens," he said, "we'll face it together."

Tears choked off any more words Carling might say. She wanted to tell her friend how much he meant to her, how much she loved him. But all she could do was cry.

The night was filled with dreams of her parents being viciously attacked by the Heilodius Centaurs. The evil eyes buried deep in the grimy face of the Centaur that had bragged about killing her mother and father kept haunting Carling as she slept. When she whimpered and cried out, Higson moved close and wrapped his cloak around her. He stroked her hair in an effort to comfort her.

Carling awoke to find her head cradled on Higson's lap. The birds and squirrels chirping and chattering in the trees overhead seemed to erase any foreboding feeling that the Forest of Rumors usually elicited as well as the painful memories of her dreams. Carling stretched her sore muscles and sat up. Her movement awoke Higson, who had been sleeping with his back resting against a tree trunk.

"Are you ready for a new day?" he mumbled groggily.

"We shall see," she replied.

Tandum and Tibbals approached. Though happy to see her friends, Carling was not happy at all to hear the filly's first words to her. "Tandum is going to take us to the hunting cottage," Tibbals said, pulling Carling to her feet.

"What if the Centaurs are still there?" Higson said, standing.

"Then we will give them what they deserve," Tandum announced boldly, his arms folded across his chest.

Still shaken from the haunting dreams that had roiled through her mind, Carling didn't know how to respond. She remembered the desire for revenge she had felt when they first came upon the murderous Centaurs. But now, her feelings were different. The craving for retaliation just wasn't there, as hard as she tried to resurrect it. She said nothing and climbed on Tibbals' back.

The two Centaurs moved through the forest but at a slower pace than the day before. Carling could tell Tibbals was still tired from the exhausting dash across the Echoing Plains. She assumed Tandum felt the same.

As they moved deeper into the forest, it became darker and quieter. Branches hung low, obscuring their view of what lay ahead. Ferns and flowers gave way to brambles and tangled weeds, concealing any sign of a path. Tandum picked the best route he could and kept them progressing. He seemed to be in possession of an internal compass that led them in the right direction. A few hours later, they stopped by the side of a stream for a much-needed break and a lunch of dried-out bread and cheese. Tibbals and Tandum let the horse part of them take over as they munched on some long grasses growing by the water's edge. Carling watched with intense curiosity, wondering how much horse and how much human went into the Centaur race. Perhaps that would be just another mystery never to be solved.

Refreshed and invigorated, Tandum trotted over. "Let's go find these Heilodius monsters," he said.

CHAPTER 21

Finding the Cabin

IT WAS NEARLY TIME for the sun to depart for the day when they reached the forest glen where the old cabin sat. All was silent. The cabin was dark. Nothing moved, other than a few branches dancing in the gentle wind.

Tandum stopped at the edge of the glen in a place where he could observe unnoticed. He listened with his keen ears, watched with his alert eyes, and sniffed the air, searching for signs of danger.

"Get down and wait here," Tandum said to Higson. The young Duende did as he was told, sliding to the ground as silently as a leaf floats to the earth in autumn.

Carling remained on Tibbals, afraid to move and certain she should not make a sound. She watched Tandum step cautiously into the clearing. With each step forward, he stopped, listened, and looked around. Seeing, hearing, and even smelling nothing, he moved forward. Step by guarded step, the colt worked his way first around the clearing, then up to the cabin. The windows were open, but the door appeared to be tightly shut. Tandum pressed his large, beautiful body against the side of the cabin, waited, then peeked in one of the windows. Straightening, he walked boldly to the front door and flung it open. He turned and, with a smile on his face, motioned for them to come.

Tibbals trotted forward, nearly unseating Carling, who was not holding on. Higson jogged along beside them.

The group entered the cabin, excited and relieved to have a warm shelter for the night. Carling dismounted and looked around her. The cabin was old but solidly built. Beds designed for Centaurs lined the walls. A water pump and bucket sat to one side of the room, waiting to be put to use. A stone fireplace filled with ashes and blackened logs stood at one end.

Unfortunately, the previous occupiers, the Heilodius Centaurs, had left quite a mess. Discarded metal bottles and scraps of food littered the floor and side tables. One lantern had been knocked off its hook, the impact of its landing on the wooden plank floor caused shards of glass to be scattered around the center of the room.

"Oh, they're disgusting," snorted Tibbals. "What a bunch of pigs."

Carling agreed but said nothing. The thought that her parents' murderers had been here made her feel a bit queasy. She decided removing the reminders of their presence would help. "Higson," she said, "will you help me clean this place up?"

Higson didn't need to reply. He stepped over to the fireplace and retrieved a brittle old broom and rusted dustpan that were resting against the stones. Handing the dustpan to Carling, he started sweeping, sending dust into the air and out the open windows while Carling tried to catch what she could.

While the Duende cleaned, the Centaurs shuffled through their packs for what remained of their food supply. In one bag they found some dried meat, in another a crust of bread. A few figs were found in the bottom of a third bag. It wasn't much, but it would be enough to quiet their grumbling stomachs. Tibbals pumped some water into metal cups and set them on the table that filled the center of the cabin.

As the sun set, the shadowy darkness that was always present in the Forest of Rumors deepened and became more menacing. Higson lit the only remaining lantern and Tandum built a fire in the stone fireplace. Carling and Tibbals went around the room, shutting windows.

The four weary travelers sat down for their meager meal, Carling and Higson on stools and Tibbals and Tandum on bed-like benches built to hold a horse's body.

Carling had just put a fig in her mouth and was savoring its sweetness when a thunderous bang shook the house and the front door crashed into the room, splintering as it hit the floor.

Before Carling even knew what was happening, Higson shoved her under the table. On her hands and knees and breathing rapidly, Carling looked out between the table legs. A dozen mud-splattered hooves stomped into the room over the broken door. She watched as they and the burly legs attached to them came to a stop.

"Well, well, well. What have we here? A feast? And you didn't have the courtesy to invite us?"

Carling's heart jumped to her throat and her pulse quickened. She knew that voice. It was the same voice that had recounted the story of the vicious killing of her mother. It was the Centaur named Clank. Her body gave an involuntary shiver.

From beneath the table, she watched the chestnut legs of Tandum unfold as he stood. "You may leave now," Tandum said boldly.

The Centaurs laughed boisterously.

"Well, I can see the king's son has inherited some of his father's arrogance!" said Clank.

"For your information," said another Centaur, "we will be sleeping here tonight. If you know what's good for you, you would leave."

Carling watched the first set of legs turn back toward the others, then heard Clank's derisive snort. "What?" he said. "You want to let them go? Don't you know who this is? These are the king's children. They are worth a lot. They can help us with our cause. We need to keep them as hostages."

The Heilodius Centaurs began debating this idea...and their other options. "Kill them," said one.

"No, we can use them," Clank repeated. "They're worth a king's ransom!"

"Let's not be bothered," another Centaur responded. "Just send them on their way,"

From her hiding place, Carling watched as Higson stood. She felt panic building inside her. She needed to remain calm and rational. She needed a plan. Her eyes darted around the room. She saw her pack with the bow and quiver of arrows resting against a bed, but it was too far for her to reach. She looked the other way and saw the sword in its leather sheath that belonged to Tandum. Again, it was too far away to be reached...unless...A plan began to take shape in her astute mind.

CHAPTER 22

Fighting the Heilodius

WHILE THE HEILODIUS CENTAURS continued arguing loudly, Carling crawled under the table and lowered
herself to her stomach. She slid between Tibbals' legs,
hoping the filly wouldn't move and step on her with her
sharp hooves. She wiggled under the bench upon which
her friend was sitting. Tibbals had chosen to sit in front
of the fire for warmth. Leaning against the stones of the
fireplace was the straw broom that Higson had used earlier. Carling kept her eyes focused on the broom and
scooted swiftly but silently toward it. Reaching it, she
grabbed hold of the bristles and pulled the broom toward
her where she lay, half concealed under the bench. She
turned the broom around until she was holding the
wooden handle. Then she slid the rest of her body out
from under the bench, hoping no one had noticed her.
Leaning forward, Carling placed the straw end of the

broom into the glowing red coals at the base of the fireplace. Immediately, the straw caught on fire and Carling jumped to her feet.

"Leave, now!" Carling ordered, jabbing the flaming broom toward the intruders.

The Heilodius Centaurs stopped their argument, whirled around, and gasped when they saw Carling coming toward them with a flaming torch. The horse half of the Centaurs was desperately afraid of fire, and this fear caused them to freeze just long enough for Higson, Tibbals, and Tandum to lunge for their weapons.

Facing a flaming torch, two swords, and a bow and arrow brought the Heilodius Centaurs to life. They reared up on their hind legs and drew swords of their own. As quick as a flash, Higson leaped to the top of the table, sending cups and dishes crashing to the ground. In one smooth motion, he pulled an arrow from his quiver, nocked it on the bow string, pulled back, and released it. Before the first Centaur, Clank, could lower his forelegs to the ground to fight, he had an arrow imbedded deep in his chest. With a scream, he collapsed to the floor.

The other two Centaurs jumped over their leader, swinging their swords over their heads. Tibbals and Tandum stepped up to meet them, blocking the downward blows with their own swords. While Tibbals whirled and kicked at the attackers with her strong hind legs, Tandum continued to fight head on.

Carling ran forward, passing Tibbals and jabbing at one Heilodius Centaur with her flaming broom. The attacker reared up again and spun on his hind legs to avoid the flames. Losing his balance on the uneven planks that formed the floor, he fell to his side, landing right on top of Clank, who was still moaning in pain. Higson jumped off the table, landing squarely on both feet. He stood his ground, his next arrow aimed at the second Centaur's heart.

Tandum still had his hands full fighting the third Heilodius herd member. Back and forth, the two moved around the room, knocking over furniture as they battled. Carling bit her lip as she watched, her heart racing. Anxious and frightened, she watched for a chance to help Tandum.

The opportunity presented itself quite by accident. Just as the two battling Centaurs came to her side of the cabin, the Heilodius Centaur whirled to avoid a lunge from Tandum's sword, sending his long black tail swishing through the flames of the burning broom Carling still held aloft. In an instant, his tail was on fire.

The Centaur screamed in terror and began running around the cabin. "Help me, help me! Clank, I'm on fire!"

Fanned by the wind the panicking Centaur was creating by running, the flames grew larger and began moving up his tail toward his body. Without considering the possible repercussions of her actions, Carling tossed her flaming broom back into the fire and ran to the bucket sitting beneath the water pump. Relieved to see it contained quite a bit of water, she snatched it up and raced toward the terrified Centaur. With a mighty swing of her arms, she sent the water sailing through the air. It splashed down on the hindquarters and tail of the creature, dousing the fire instantly.

The Centaur stopped in his tracks and turned back to look at his once-beautiful tail, which was now dripping water from a few spindly strands. But he was alive, and when he looked back at Carling, his eyes reflected that realization. He dropped his sword. "You saved me. Why?" he asked. "You should have let me die."

Carling began to open her mouth to speak, but had no words to say. She just shook her head.

Tibbals came up to her and put her arms around her shoulders. "It's the Stone of Mercy," she whispered in her ear.

Carling looked up into her beautiful friend's face and shrugged. Something had made her save the Centaur, but she couldn't really articulate what. It was as though she'd been moved by some magical power that had taken control of her. Something like the power that had moved her to save the Faun. Surely Tibbals was right: this was the result of the Stone of Mercy.

Carling turned her attention to the three injured Heilodius Centaurs. "Your lives have been spared," she said, sounding like the queen she was to become. "But there must be a balance between justice and mercy. You will have to pay for the crimes you have committed. You murdered my parents and destroyed the village of Duenton. We will take you back there to stand trial for your terrible deeds. But you will live, a gift you denied my mother and father."

From where he lay on the floor, Clank pushed himself up on his arms. A pool of blood was forming around his front hooves. His eyes narrowed and with clenched teeth he said, "I will never stand before your courts. You have no authority over me!"

Tandum stepped up to him. "Oh, we don't? That's a fine way to show your gratitude to someone for sparing your life."

"I would rather die than pay venerations to a Duende," he spat out.

Calmly Carling walked over to stand beside Tandum. "You have a debt to pay," she said, addressing Clank, "and we will see to it that you do."

"We shall see," Clank sneered before turning away.

CHAPTER 23

The Storm

FOR THE NEXT COUPLE of hours, Carling and Higson set about tending to any wounds that had been suffered by the Centaurs. When everyone was bandaged up and the Heilodius Centaurs were restrained with hobbles, fed what little was still available, and given water and a place to lie down, the Duende and the Minsheen Centaurs set about repairing the damaged door. Using rope found in the cabin, they tied the door back in place and latched it securely shut. Content with their work, they made themselves comfortable for the few hours that remained of the night.

Clank and his cohorts lay still and silent in one corner, speaking neither to one another nor to their young captors.

The morning sun was covered by a thick blanket of clouds. A blustery wind buffeted the cabin, waking its occupants. Soon, large balls of hail drummed against the wooden shake roof, filling the inside with so much noise Carling could barely hear anything else. She looked around and noticed the others wearing expressions of concern, mirroring her own feelings. She got up and started a fire, but the wind that hurled down the chimney blew the smoke into the room. With eyes stinging and coughing loudly, she doused the embryonic flames with water from the pump. "No hot water for us," she said to no one in particular, which was good because no one could hear her anyway.

Higson got out of bed. "What can I do to help you?" he asked, shouting above the sound of the hail.

"We need to find something to eat. Any ideas?"

Tibbals unfolded her long legs and lowered her hooves to the floor. "I don't have anything left in my pack," she said with a frown.

"Nor do I," Tandum yelled from the far side of the room.

The Heilodius Centaurs continued to lie silently in a corner of the room. Clank only glared at his captors. Apparently, they had nothing to contribute, either.

"Well," said Carling, pulling the pump handle up and pushing it down again. "It looks like all we have is water."

"I hope we don't have to go out in this terrible storm," said Tibbals, pulling her hair to the side of her head and plaiting the blond tresses into a long braid. The braid finished, she examined her fingernails and frowned.

Tandum walked to a window and looked out. The trees were swaying violently from side to side; branches were breaking off and hurling through the air. Above, the clouds rolled by in anger. He turned back around and faced his fellow travelers. "We won't be going anywhere until this storm blows over."

"We'll starve if we have to stay here long," Carling said, feeling her stomach grumble.

"I could go out and try to hunt for something," offered Higson.

Tandum shook his head. "There won't be any animals out in this weather. They'll all be hiding in their burrows and nests."

Carling put a hand on Higson's shoulder. "I would rather starve than have you out in this storm. We'll just rest in here for as long as we need to. Save up your energy."

"She's right," chimed in Tibbals. "We'll be on our way soon. And we're only a day's journey from home. Surely we can get by without food for just a day."

The violent storm continued for much longer than the group anticipated, however. Wind and hail beat against the cabin windows, as though trying desperately to get inside. Occasionally a branch from a nearby tree broke loose and slammed against the side of the cabin, making everyone jump. The Minsheen Centaurs and the Duende talked about being hungry, but not about much else. Mostly, they just sat, wrapped in blankets, and waited.

As she relaxed on one of the beds, her chin resting on her knees, Carling looked over at Clank and his companions where they sat bound in their corner. Clank was staring at her, his eyes cold and hard. Curiosity overcame her and she asked, "Clank, why did you join the Heilodius herd?"

"And just why shouldn't I have?" he said with a sneer.

"Couldn't the Centaurs negotiate a peaceful agreement with the other races if they remained one unified herd?" Carling continued, ignoring his retort. "There is power in numbers."

Clank snorted. "You think you can just waltz up to a Cyclops, shake hands, smile, and walk away with the throne? If you think that, you are stupider than I thought."

His two companions snickered.

"Why does there have to be just one ruler of Crystonia?" Carling asked. "Why can't there be a representative from each race?"

"You mean rule by committee? That is the most ridiculous thing I have ever heard."

"Why is it so ridiculous?" Carling prodded, sincerely wanting an answer.

"Because committees never get anything accomplished. They just argue back and forth. Eventually, someone has to rise to the top and take the lead. The strongest is the one that obtains leadership."

"Or wisest?"

"Strongest," Clank repeated for emphasis. "And I intend to be on the side of the strongest when the power is divvied out. Now quit talking to me. You bore me," he said, turning his head to one side.

"We should have killed them when we had the chance," said Tandum, shaking his head and frowning.

Hearing this comment, Clank looked up. "That was a decision you will live to regret."

Carling sighed and smoothed the wrinkled tunic that covered her silver breastplate. She had a lot to learn, she concluded. Silence once again filled the room.

Late in the afternoon, Carling was dozing, leaning against Higson, when she was jarred awake by a loud pounding on the door. Everyone looked up, eyes wide with surprise and concern. Tandum unfolded his legs and stepped off his bed. Carling watched him as he slowly, cautiously, crossed the room and approached the door. With his hand on the door latch, he looked back at her, as if asking for permission to open it. More loud bangs were heard by all over the howling of the storm. Crank and his friends looked back and forth at each other and exchanged sardonic smiles. Tandum raised the latch and the door burst open, pushed by the wind.

Standing on the wooden porch, soaking wet and covered with mud, leaves, and pine needles, were the Fauns who had captured Higson, Tibbals, and Tandum. Pik stumbled into the room. Shivering violently, he said, "Can we s-s-stay here?"

In the next instant, a dozen more Fauns pushed their way into the little cabin, filling it with the foul smell of wet animals and covering the floorboards with mud and water. Clank frowned.

"Pik!" exclaimed Carling, truly shocked to see him. "Of course you can stay with us. But, please, shut the door!"

The Fauns in the back grunted as they strained to shut the door against the wind that was trying to bully them. It took three Fauns to get the door closed and bolted.

The little cabin now held two little Duende; two Centaurs from the Minsheen herd; three Centaurs from the Heilodius herd; and twelve very wet, cold, and dirty Fauns.

The Tables Are Turned

CARLING DIDN'T SLEEP THAT night, having spent much of the day asleep. At first she just lay awake, listening to the seemingly endless storm. But sometime during the night, the storm ran its course. The wind, hail, and rain stopped. Carling felt her body relax with relief. But the sounds of the storm were replaced by the rumbling snores of a dozen exhausted Fauns deep in sleep.

"Carling, are you awake?" she heard Higson whisper.

"Are you kidding? How could I sleep with all that racket?"

Carling heard Higson chuckle. "You're right there, you are," he responded.

"At least the storm seems to have passed."

"Good, that. I want to get home. I'm starving!"

"Higson?" she said, still whispering.

"Yes?"

"Thank you for helping me."

"You know I'd do anything for you."

"You say that now, but what if things get even more dangerous? Remember what the Wizard said?"

Higson didn't hesitate. "It doesn't matter what comes our way. We will face it together."

Carling smiled as she looked over at the window. She could see just a hint of moonlight weaving through the trees. For a moment, she forgot her hunger as she was filled with gratitude for her friend and his generosity. Then the warmth of that moment passed and she felt her body tighten. She clenched her jaw and curled her hands into tight fists. *What am I doing to him?* she asked herself. *What have I gotten him into? I can't ask him to risk his life for me.* She turned onto her side so she was facing Higson. Her voice quivering, the young Duende spoke so softly that it was surprising that he even heard her. "I can't do that to you," she said. "I love you too much."

"And I love you," her friend replied. "That is why it doesn't matter if you ask me or not. I will be at your side, come what may."

Everyone woke in the morning grouchy and hungry. The prospect of the long journey that awaited them didn't make anyone feel any better. The one bright spot to the day was brought to them by the warm sunlight that sifted through the windows. Sunshine has a way of worming its way into everyone's heart, especially after a wild, tempestuous storm like the one that had just passed.

Carling stepped onto the cabin's tiny porch and threw out her arms to embrace the day. Tibbals appeared at the front door. "The forest doesn't seem as foreboding after it's been given a good washing," she said with a smile.

Carling stroked her friend's golden shoulder. "You're right there," she said.

Tandum soon joined them. "So, what shall we do with all these prisoners we seem to have collected on this journey?"

Carling and Tibbals laughed, and then Tibbals looked down at Carling. She raised her eyebrows and cocked her head.

Carling ran her fingers through her long, thick hair. "Well, the Heilodius can keep up with us. The Fauns...they will have to continue making their way to Duenton on their own as quickly as they can."

Having no reason to stay in the cabin any longer and eager to get home and put some food in their stomachs, the companions set out through the Forest of Rumors. Tandum and Higson led the way, pulling on the ropes that held their three prisoners bound. Carling, on Tibbals, brought up the rear. They moved slowly through the muddy paths. The tree branches hung low, heavy with water that dripped on the travelers until they were soaked through their cloaks. It was miserable going, even with the occasional ray of sunlight that made its way through the shadows.

As they struggled along, Carling noticed how quiet the forest was. No birds or squirrels chattered in the treetops. The only sound she heard was the sucking sound of hooves sinking into and pulling out of the mud. The silence was ominous.

They traveled what must have been only an hour when an ear splitting crack filled the silence. With a rumble and a crash, a giant tree smashed to the ground, barely missing Tandum who had to jump back to get out of the way of its flailing branches. The trail in front of them was now blocked by the fallen tree.

The Heilodius Centaurs, who up until this time had trudged along silently, seemed to perk up. "What's the matter, oh great colt of a king?" said Clank, his voice thick with condescension. "You can't let a little tree stop you."

Tandum ignored him as Tibbals stepped up to look over the situation. Just as she reached her brother's side, however, a heavy net made of vines dropped over both them and their riders. A half dozen Centaurs appeared from behind the trees surrounding them and were soon pulling and tying the net tightly around the torsos of the foursome.

As Tandum and Higson pushed at the net, Carling and Tibbals clutched at it. They were all trapped. Above the commotion that surrounded them, Carling picked out Clank's laughter as clearly as an orchestra conductor hears an individual viola.

"What took you so long?" Clank said once he got a hold of himself.

"Sorry, boss," responded one of the Centaurs timidly. "That storm yesterday really messed things up."

"Well, never mind. Make sure they're tied up good!"

Tandum and Higson continued to struggle against the net that held them so tightly. The ropes, that were now wound around them all, bound their arms to their sides and kept them from being able to reach their weapons.

Carling sat quietly on Tibbals, no longer grasping the net that covered her and her friends as her mind searched for answers to this sudden quagmire. Why hadn't she realized there would be more Heilodius herd members out here in the forest? She hadn't even thought to inquire of her prisoners where the others they'd seen on their way to Manyon Canyon were now. Of course, they probably wouldn't have told her, but at least she should have been on guard. Now they were captives and were greatly outnumbered.

"Let's get moving," shouted Clank.

With shouts and tugs on the ropes, the Heilodius Centaurs turned Tibbals and Tandum and their riders to the north. Pushed and prodded with the points of swords, the Minsheen Centaurs were forced to move through the forest at a trot. Even Clank, with his injuries, seemed to be having little trouble keeping up a fast pace.

Their captors turned away from Tandum's intended route, moving in a northern direction. The forest smelled of wet dirt and dripping pine trees. Steam arose from the ground as the sun evaporated the moisture from the storm, making the Heilodius Centaurs seem like eerie flickers of Carling's imagination.

"I'm getting really tired of being tied up with ropes," said Tibbals, turning as best she could to look back at Carling and giving her a forced smile.

Carling sympathetically patted her friend's side. She wasn't sure what to say. Fear was beginning to take hold of her heart in its cold, cruel fist. Tibbals' attempt at a joke was welcome but did little to ease the flow of ice that was pulsing through Carling's veins. *Where are they taking us? What's going to happen to us once we get there?* she wondered.

Tandum took the issue head on. "Where do you think you are taking us?" he demanded.

One of the Centaurs who was pulling the ropes jerked on the bindings even harder before responding. "We don't think nothin'. We know!"

"And that would be....?" probed Tandum.

"We're headed back to our city."

"You mean on the slopes of Mount Heilodius?" Tandum responded. The look on his face showed his surprise.

"That's the only city I know of," sneered another.

"But why?" Tandum asked.

"You've been causing too much trouble."

"What do you mean, *we* have been causing trouble?" Tibbals added, nearly in tears. "You started this when you tried to kidnap me!"

"Yeah. Then these two pipsqueaks had to stick their noses in where they don't belong," added one as he glared at Carling and poked her with a spear.

"Leave her alone," shouted Higson.

"Oh, aren't you the brave little one!" mocked the offending Centaur. "It don't look to me like you're in any position to protect her." All of the Heilodius Centaurs around them laughed.

"Enough of this banter," shouted Clank over his shoulder. "Just keep moving." The Centaurs quieted immediately and refocused their attention on weaving through the forest.

At a trot, the group covered a lot of ground quickly. They eventually reached the edge of the forest. Carling looked ahead and saw the massive outline of Mount Heilodius, its peak piercing the clouds and disappearing from sight. It was the closest and the tallest peak in the ridge of mountains that formed the northern boundary of Crystonia, the region called The Northern Reaches.

The appearance of the mountain and the open plains seemed to energize the Heilodius Centaurs, who quickly picked up their pace to a rolling canter. Tibbals and Tandum had no choice but to canter as well as they could.

The looming mountain grew larger as they moved toward it. The details of its shape and the trees and cliffs that covered its surface became clearer. Carling had never seen such an imposing peak and wondered that it could look both ominous and beautiful. She stared at it, her violet eyes wide with wonder. The thought that she was destined to rule from this mountain was so overwhelming, she had to push it out of her head. Yet, she could not deny that some strange force was pulling her toward it.

"Tibbals," Carling whispered. "If Mount Heilodius is supposed to be the site of the ruler of Crystonia, has the Heilodius herd taken control of the capital and the throne?"

"Oh, no," the filly answered. "The Heilodius herd has built a city at the base of the mountain in an attempt to block anyone from ascending the mountain's slopes and taking possession of the throne."

"Enough talking," one of the guards snarled as he poked Tibbals in the haunches. "Keep moving."

Carling turned and glared at him. "You don't have to treat her like that."

"Keep up and I won't," was the curt response.

The prisoners and their guards reached the shore of an expansive lake just as the sun was setting. Mount Heilodius, which was directly across the lake, was reflected in the still, slate-gray waters. A large fish broke through the surface of the lake to catch a low-flying moth and immediately disappeared back into the depths of the lake.

"We'll stop here for the night," Clank barked. The Centaurs of both herds breathed a sigh of relief. They were all exhausted. Carling and Higson sat, slumped over on the Minsheen Centaur's backs, waiting to be untied so they could dismount. They were hungry and thirsty and the water in the lake was inviting.

Unfortunately, the Heilodius Centaurs were not concerned with the welfare of their captives. Those holding the ropes that held Tibbals, Tandum, and their riders tied them to two trees set just far enough back from the shoreline that they could not reach the water. The Heilodius Centaurs trotted into the lake, where they bent over and scooped handfuls of water into their mouths. Carling watched, her mouth and throat dry, her body yearning for water and nourishment. Initially she was patient, sure that her captors would, at the very least, let her dismount and go to the water.

Once the Centaurs had drunk their fill, however, they built a campfire and settled down around it. Several opened their packs and passed around rolls, cheese, and dried meats. Carling watched with angst. She had not eaten in two days, and her body was weak from hunger. Her stomach growled in protest.

Tibbals stood stiffly, watching and waiting as well. When no one made the effort to even let them drink, Tibbals spoke up. "Excuse me, excuse me," she said in an attempt to get someone's attention. When no one acknowledged hearing her, she shouted. "We are still tied up over here and can't get to the water. Would someone please untie us?"

Clank was sitting a short distance away with two of his companions, the ones who had been in the cabin with him. He turned to look over at his captives and raised his eyebrows. "Do you have some sort of problem?" he asked.

Tibbals lifted her chin. "Yes. I'm very tired, very thirsty, and very hungry." Her pouting lips curled petulantly.

"Do you think that is my problem? When you had us tied up in the corner of the cabin, you didn't feed us anything."

Carling felt her patience rush out of her like the wind across the prairie. "We shared the very little we had and gave you plenty of water," she said, trying to keep her voice under control.

"Well, we don't have enough to share with you, so you'll just have to get used to being hungry. We aren't your servants, after all," Clank responded before turning back to the fire.

When the Centaur with the burnt-off tail looked over at Carling, she thought she saw sympathy in his eyes...but decided she'd been wrong when he, too, turned back to the fire.

Resigned to their hunger and thirst, Tibbals and Tandum folded their long legs and lay down beneath the trees to which they were tied. Carling and Higson did their best to wiggle around the ropes and maneuver off their friends' backs so they could rest.

The Heilodius Centaurs soon fell asleep. Carling watched the tiny sparks float up into the air like little fireflies, wishing she and her friends were close enough to benefit from any warmth the fire might offer. Just as she was about to close her eyes and try to sleep, she noticed one of the Centaurs lift his head and look over at her. It was the Centaur with the burnt tail. She cocked her head, curious, as he unfolded his legs and stood. Slowly and cautiously, he picked his way around the sleeping bodies of the other guards, carefully placing his hooves on the ground so as not to make any noise. At one of the packs, he bent down and shuffled through its contents until he pulled out a bowl. Turning toward Carling, he placed his finger to his lips, warning her to be quiet. He walked over to the lake and scooped up some water.

Carling licked her lips with her dry, swollen tongue, holding her breath in eager anticipation. But when the Centaur arrived and extended his arm to pass her the water, she shook her head. "Tibbals," she whispered as she gently shook her friend's arm. Tibbals raised her head, her golden locks falling over her face. "Tibbals, water."

Tibbals brushed aside her hair and looked eagerly around. Seeing the bowl being proffered to her, she squealed with delight. "Sh-h-h-h-h," hushed Carling and the Centaur together.

Tibbals took the bowl and brought it to her lips. She drank until it was empty, then sighed with relief as the refreshing water flowed through her.

One by one, each of the captives drank the water the Centaur brought to them. This simple act of kindness would never be forgotten by the four, even as Carling's kind act that saved his own life would never be forgotten by the Centaur.

CHAPTER 25

Rescue the Enemy

THE WATER TRICKED CARLING'S stomach into thinking she had eaten, relieving the pain in her belly long enough for her to relax, close her eyes, and sleep.

Just before dawn, the time when all is silent and nothing moves, when the world seems to be waiting for the sunlight to bring everything back to life, Carling woke with a start. She looked around her and noticed that she appeared to be the only one awake. She wondered what had brought her out of her deep sleep.

As the high screech of a raptor echoed through the trees, Carling realized what had awakened her. She knew instinctively that the cry was from an eagle, and not just any eagle. It was from Baskus. A tinge of excitement entered her heart. She looked from one treetop to the next, her eyes squinting as she searched for him. A sudden movement caught her attention and she turned to one side. Seated on a sturdy pine branch far above Carling,

Baskus was tilting his head and looking down at her with one of his dark, round eyes.

Carling lifted one delicate hand and waved at him, a smile filling her face as hope filled her heart. But the hope suddenly disappeared along with the smile as she watched the giant bird lift off and disappear in the early morning sky. She wanted to cry out to him to come back, but she feared waking the guards. Instead, she bit her lip and let the tears that were stinging her eyes roll down her cheeks.

By the time the Heilodius herd had fixed themselves some breakfast, the sun was well off the eastern horizon. Carling watched them eat and drink, her stomach churning, her parched throat aching. She looked over at Higson, sure he was feeling the same, and offered him an encouraging smile. He didn't return it.

"Let's get moving," shouted Clank. "I want to get to Fort Heilodius by mid-afternoon."

"Clank, shouldn't we give the prisoners something to eat?" It was the Centaur with the burnt tail.

Clank rolled his eyes and shook his head in apparent disgust. The leader of the band glared at this minion for a few moments, appearing to consider his options. Finally he said, "Give them water but nothing else."

Grateful for the water but still weak from hunger, Carling, Higson, Tibbals, and Tandum began their journey around the shore of Lake Mantle.

"I've heard of this lake," said Tibbals as they trudged along. "I've never seen it before. I had no idea it was so enormous."

"It captures the snow melt off Mount Heilodius," Tandum said without looking up. "That's where it gets its name: Mantle. The snow flows down like an emperor's mantle. Today it looks calm and peaceful, but I have heard that it becomes a wild monster in a storm. Many a fisherman has lost his life trying to compete with her fury."

Fascinated, Carling gazed over the sparkling water turned blue by the reflection of the sky. *What would it be like to sail across her turquoise waters?* she asked herself. On this day, it was impossible to imagine Lake Mantle being anything but welcoming.

The sun warmed the air, making it increasingly difficult to keep moving. Even the Heilodius Centaurs begged Clank for a rest...something he refused to grant. Carling stared at his back, sure that his wound from their battle in the cabin must still be hurting him. Yet strength combined with stubbornness kept him moving toward his destination.

With each of their long strides, the Minsheen Centaurs and their riders moved farther and farther from their home. Carling thought of this and felt her body tense. Knowing this must be uncomfortable for Tibbals, however, she tried to relax. But before long, she felt her body get tight again.

As they moved along, Carling kept gazing up at the sapphire sky, hoping to see Baskus. When he didn't appear, she began to doubt the eagle she'd seen had been him at all. Hopelessness began to fill her heart.

Some stretches of the trail they were following meandered lazily along the lake's shoreline. In other places, it climbed along the side of steep cliffs. At these places, the group was forced to move in single file as the trail was terribly narrow. It was so narrow, in fact, that Carling scrapped her leg along the upward side of the cliff.

"Ouch," she mumbled through gritted teeth.

"I'm so sorry," Tibbals apologized.

"Don't worry. Just keep us on the trail," said Carling, looking to the other side where a steep descent ended in the lake far below. "I'd rather get a few scrapes than fall down there."

No sooner had she said that than a shout and a scream were heard coming from behind them. Tibbals stopped and both she and Carling turned their heads just in time to see one of the Heilodius Centaurs scrambling desperately in an attempt to keep from falling down the cliff. His efforts were futile and he started falling, bouncing and crashing down the side of the rocky ledge. With a splash, he landed in the water of the lake, sending a ring of ripples out in all directions. Everyone stood with mouths agape and eyes open in shock. For a moment, no one moved.

As soon as Carling was able to register what had just happened, she called out, "We need to help him! Get these ropes off Tibbals and me and we will save him!"

"Oh, no, you don't," shouted Clank.

"But he's drowning!" answered Tibbals.

"I don't much care about him. I'm not releasing you."

"Clank," pleaded Carling. "Tibbals and I promise to come back. Please untie us and we will use the ropes to rescue your friend."

"Who said he was my friend?" sneered Clank, showing his true character.

"Dalt is my friend," the Centaur with the burnt tail answered softly. Without saying anything else, the Centaur pivoted his four feet carefully around on the narrow trail and moved over to Carling and Tibbals.

As he was untying the ropes, Clank started yelling. "Bale, if you release them, I'll make sure you spend the rest of your life behind bars with them."

Carling looked deeply into Bale's eyes. "We will come back. I give you my word. Thank you for helping us save your friend."

The Centaur nodded. "Good luck, and thank you."

As soon as the ropes were loosened, Carling wound them into several long loops. "Let's go, Tibbals."

"Hold on, Carling," the filly said as she turned toward the edge of the cliff.

Suddenly realizing what his sister was about to do, Tandum shouted in alarm, "Don't do it, Tibbals!"

Too late. With a strong push from her hindquarters, Tibbals leaped off the narrow ridge that formed the path, flew through the air, and landed with a loud splash in the lake.

As soon as Tibbals and Carling hit the water, they went far under. Carling was shocked at how cold the lake was. She left the filly's back and swam to the surface. As soon as her face broke through, she looked around while gasping for breath. She saw the cliff and the point where the Centaur had gone under a short distance away. Wasting no time, she started swimming toward the spot where she believed the Centaur to be. Tibbals also came up and started swimming in the same direction.

It took only a few minutes for them to reach their targeted spot. The Centaur that had fallen was nowhere to be seen.

"I'm going under to see if I can find him," huffed Carling, unaccustomed to swimming, even in warm water.

"I'm going with you."

Each of them sucked in as much air as they could and dove under the water.

The water was clear and the rocks that covered the edge of the lake nearest the cliff were quite visible. Just to their left, both girls saw the body of the Centaur. Together, they came up for another breath of air.

"Let's tie the rope around his front legs and chest and try to get him to the surface," shouted Carling between sucking in deep breaths.

Tibbals nodded and they both swam down again. While Carling wrapped the rope under the Centaur's front legs, Tibbals worked to secured the other end around his chest. Carling pulled on the ropes in an attempt to bring the Centaur up to the surface. The Centaur felt like an anchor, holding Carling in place underwater. She kicked her legs hard, but he didn't budge. Grasping the rope, she pulled with all her might, grateful when Tibbals joined in and the Centaur's body began to move slightly.

Looking up, Carling could see the blue sky overhead, but the surface of the water seemed so far away. *I don't know if I can do this*, she said to herself as she released the last of the air she'd been holding in her lungs. Carling could feel her lungs burning as they pleaded for more air and she began to feel a bit light-headed. She kept pulling, even as her flagging strength began to flow out of her and float away. When she heard the loud reverberation of something splashing into the lake, she worried that Clank had ordered his ranks to try to kill her and Tibbals by dropping boulders onto them.

Just as Carling was about to give up, she became aware of someone else beside her. Higson grasped the rope and motioned for her to go to the surface. She let go and swam as quickly as she could until her head popped out of the water. Gasping and choking, she began treading water while she tried to feed air to her starving lungs. Almost immediately, Higson, Tibbals, and Tandum surfaced and began pulling the ropes until the injured Centaur rose to the top of the lake. Carling pointed to the sandy beach that had been formed by a swirling eddy just ahead. By unspoken consent, the four rescuers began pulling the Centaur through the water toward the tiny beach.

It took all four of them to pull the dying creature out of the water. Carling looked down at him and felt dread fill her. It seemed they were too late to save him, that all of this had been for naught. But Tandum began pressing on his chest anyway. Carling collapsed against the rock face of the cliff in exhaustion and watched Tandum, the veins on her head pulsing as her heart battled to pump blood through her weak and tired body.

When Tandum became worn-out, Higson took over. High above, the Heilodius Centaurs watched, some amazed and awed by the bravery and selflessness of their prisoners. Others, like Clank, were convinced the Minsheen Centaurs and Duende were the most foolish creatures they had ever seen.

Just after Higson fell back on his heels in exhaustion and Tandum resumed pressing on the Centaur's chest, the injured soldier began coughing. Tandum leaned back as the Centaur vomited up his morning meal and began moaning.

"Tandum and Higson, you did it!" Tibbals cried out.

Tandum and Higson, too tired to respond, watched Dalt as he struggled to breathe on his own.

"Hey you up there," shouted Tibbals, addressing the Heilodius Centaurs above them. "We need some bandages. Toss down my pack."

One of the Centaurs disappeared and then reappeared with her pack, which he lowered on a rope. Tibbals grabbed it even before it reached the ground. Carling struggled to her feet and helped Tibbals tear one of her tunics into strips of fabric and bind them around the Centaur's many wounds. Between gritted teeth Tibbals said, "This was one of my favorite blouses. I hope he appreciates this."

Looking like a mummified monster, Dalt tried to respond to their kind treatment. "How can I ever thank you for saving my life?"

"How about letting us go?" said Tibbals, not really expecting that would happen.

"I-I-I don't know if I can do that. B-b-but I will do my best to see that you are treated k-k-kindly...at least I'll try," he said, stumbling over each word as he tried to catch his breath and remain conscious.

As the Duende and Centaurs struggled to get the injured guard up the cliff and back to the trail, an enormous eagle swooped low over the lake, grabbed a fish with its talons, and flew off again. Had Carling noted the eagle's identity, a glimmer of hope might have replaced the dread and discouragement she felt as she and her friends returned to their captors.

CHAPTER 26

Fort Heilodius

WHEN THEY MANAGED, WITH tremendous effort, to get the injured guard up to the trail, Clank approached them. The Centaur stood in front of them, his jaw clenched, his hands in fists pressed against his waist. He stomped his front hooves and swished his tail. He was noticeably infuriated by the delay and the disobedience of some of his company.

Carling ignored it.

"Tie up the prisoners," he shouted. The guards were quick to obey and Carling and Higson were tied, once again, onto Tibbals and Tandum with thick ropes. More ropes encircled the Minsheen Centaurs.

"Let's get moving! We've wasted far too much time already," bellowed Clank as he moved to the front of the line. Before striking off, he turned his head and shoulders back and glared at the wounded Centaur. "Dalt, keep up if you can and try to stay on the trail from now on." Clank began marching rhythmically toward Fort Heilodius as the rest of the little army fell into step. The injured Centaur was left behind to do his best to limp home.

Carling could tell Clank really didn't care what happened to the Centaur named Dalt. She kept looking back over her shoulder as the line of Centaurs got farther and farther away from the injured guard. Her heart ached, but she was helpless to do anything more to help him.

The sun had passed its zenith when the group rounded the eastern shore of the lake. Carling squinted as they marched toward the sun. Within the hour, the walls of a great fort came into view. The entire stronghold was contained behind a wall of thick timbers. The wall was so high, no buildings were visible, but arrow slits chiseled out every so often for viewing and defending were evident. Fort Heilodius looked formidable.

In the center of the south wall, a large iron gate guarded the entrance to the city. It was currently raised, but several Centaurs in the black tunics of the Heilodius herd, holding bows with arrows nocked, stood guard. Recognizing Clank, they lowered their arrows, nodded their heads, and let them all enter. The guards' eyes zeroed in on Carling and Higson, examining them closely as they passed.

Carling felt their eyes piercing her and a shiver went through her body. Tibbals must have felt it, for she said, "We'll be okay, Carling. Don't worry." Carling couldn't tell if her friend really believed that or not, but she appreciated her effort to offer comfort.

Once they got past the fort entrance, the group entered a large courtyard. Several Heilodius Centaurs in their black uniforms were marching in formation, their hooves clanging on the stones that covered the open space.

Around the square, shabbily built structures leaned against one another, holding each other up. Some appeared to be shops that sold armaments and other supplies, while others were inns offering food and drinks. Drinks, mostly.

Clank led them on a circuitous route, circumventing the military drills, until they were on the opposite side of the courtyard. Here, he headed up a narrow passageway. As they passed the villagers, most of them stallions, Carling couldn't help but notice the sorrowful, downtrodden appearance of everyone they saw. The mares seemed especially demoralized. There was only sadness in their downcast eyes. Carling tried to reach them with the only thing she had to offer: a smile. Nothing was offered in return.

The winding street took them to a building of much more substance than the sloppily constructed shacks that lined the square. This building was made of irregular stones in shades of brown and gray that appeared to have been hastily but securely fitted together. The roof was covered with pieces of slate in dark and light gray. No windows adorned the walls on this side of the garrison. Guards were visible as they marched across the rooftop. Watchmen stood stiff and straight on either side of another iron door built into the lower level of the edifice. Carling found it hard to believe that the same race that had created the magnificent city of Minsheen would also have created the collection of hovels they'd just passed as well as this monstrosity. The lack of artistry and craftsmanship should have offended her Duende blood. Instead, the sight of this imposing, massive structure filled her with nothing but dread.

Clank halted in front of the heavy, solid door. "We desire to see the Commander."

"Your business?" asked one of the guards.

Clank's mouth curled into a sneer as he snarled, "We have valuable prisoners to turn over to him."

"Wait here." One of the watchmen opened the iron door and disappeared into the foreboding building.

Clank growled under his breath and started pacing. Carling let her eyes follow him, convinced that impatience and pride would surely one day contribute to his downfall. She realized she was actually feeling sorry for him. Her hand flew to her chest and she pressed the feeling deep inside. She didn't want to feel any compassion for such a terrible creature...the creature that had killed her parents and then laughed about it. She felt a tear trickle down her cheek and leave a salty trail on her skin.

The door swung open and the watchman stepped out. With a sweeping motion of his arm, he said, "The Commander will see you now."

Head and chin high, Clank stomped past him as he led his band of followers into the citadel.

The large room they entered was windowless. An overhead chandelier of candles provided the only light. The air was thick and heavy and smelled of damp mold and mildew. The Centaurs' hooves clattered on the rough stone floor. They were missing the disciplined, rhythmic marching of the solders drilling in the square. It occurred to Carling that she may have been taken captive by a ragtag vigilante group.

They wound their way down several curving halls, past closed doors and open stairways. Carling and Higson had dismounted from their Centaurs, and now Carling walked beside Tibbals in silence. Wondering what her friend might be thinking, she looked up at her, but Tibbals was looking straight ahead, her jaw clenched.

Taking her eyes off where she was headed proved to be a poor decision for Carling as her foot caught the sharp edge of a stone in the uneven floor. She fell forward with a cry, catching herself with her hands and scraping her palms and knees.

Higson was immediately by her side. "Carling! Are you alright?"

Before Carling could answer, Clank turned around. "Get up and get moving!"

Higson helped her up and watched with concern on his face as Carling brushed herself off. They continued on. They had no other choice.

At last they stopped in front of a set of double doors set into an arched entryway. Clank pounded loudly on the thick planks of wood. Hoof beats were heard coming toward the door. With a creak of rusty hinges and the scrape of wood on stone, the door opened.

"You may enter," the Centaur who'd opened the door said, glaring at them.

Carling wondered why everyone at Fort Heilodius seemed so angry.

Once through the doorway, Carling and her companions found themselves in a large, windowless room. A fireplace at the side provided some welcome warmth, and tapestries depicting Centaurs in battle added some color and even softness to the stone walls.

Directly in front of them was a piece of furniture that could only be described as a throne. It stood on a raised dais. Lounging across the long padded cushions of the throne was the largest Centaur Carling had ever seen. His body was brown and a long, black tail curled around in front of him, lying across his folded legs.

The human-like part of the huge Centaur's body was covered with the black tunic Carling recognized as the uniform preferred by the Heilodius herd. It covered a chest of bulging muscles. However, this tunic was also decorated with a sparkling silver insignia of a crown encircled by stars. The Centaur's hair was as silver as the symbol on his chest. His dark eyes peered at them beneath bushy silver eyebrows. His strong, square jaw was clean shaven, and his thin lips were pressed into a straight line.

As soon as she entered the room, Tibbals gasped and grabbed Tandum's arm. "Uncle," she whispered. Carling heard this and remembered Tandum telling her that their uncle had disappeared and his whereabouts were unknown.

Their uncle's strong arms held a silver scepter that he lowered until it was pointing directly at the intruders. "For what purpose have you disturbed me?" he asked, his voice deep and gravelly.

Clank stepped in front of the group and bowed. "Commander, we have taken these members of the Minsheen herd and these Duende captive. We brought them to you to decide their fate."

"And just what possessed you to capture them?" the Commander asked.

Clank spun around and grabbed Carling and Higson. He shoved them forward. "These two Duende are responsible for an attack on my men."

Carling looked up at Clank, then back at the Commander. "We were only trying to protect the young fillies who were being abducted by him and his men," she said, lifting her chin and staring directly into the leader's dark eyes.

"Well, a spunky one. I like that," he said, raising one eyebrow as his mouth lifted into half a smile.

"Clank had no business capturing us," added Higson. "We have done nothing wrong."

"I would not be so quick to assert your innocence, young Duende," the Commander said. "Interfering in our activities is grounds enough to justify your capture. Clank and his men had every right to retaliate."

"By whose laws?" roared Tandum. All eyes turned to the young Centaur.

"Well, well, well. What have we here?" sneered the Commander, apparently noticing Tandum for the first time. "Is not this the son of the Minsheen stallion, the infamous Manti?"

"I am," Tandum replied. "And I demand that you order your men to release us at once so we may return to our home. We have been brought here against our will."

Tibbals stepped up beside her brother and the Commander looked over at her with both surprise and admiration in his eyes. "Oh, my! Oh, my, indeed! Now this is a pleasant surprise. The prince and princess have left their palace on high and condescended to mingle with the commoners. Learning about the real world, are we?"

Ignoring his insults, Tibbals spoke. "I know who you are," said Tibbals. "You are our father's brother. You are our uncle."

A smiled formed slowly across the Commander's face. "Yes. I am glad you recognize me. It saves time not having to deal with introductions after all."

Tibbals spoke again, her voice quivering only slightly. "When our father learns of this, there will be severe consequences."

The Commander laughed. "Oh-h-h-h, I am so frightened of my dear, dear brother. What to do? What to do?" His fingers stroked the silver scepter. "I guess the only answer is to make sure my worthless, spineless brother doesn't learn of your fate." His voice rose in volume. "Put them in the prison cells!"

"No!" shouted Carling. "You have no need of them. I am the one you want," she said as she tore open her cloak. "Behold, I wear the silver breastplate."

The Heilodius Centaurs all gasped and stepped back.

The Commander unfolded his long legs and stood up. At first he only stared at her. Then he stepped forward and walked slowly around her. Carling felt an icy terror sprout in her chest and bloom like a cancerous tumor. But she remained standing in place, her head held high.

At last, the Commander stopped circling and stood directly in front of her. His keen eyes inspected her face. "So, Clank, not only have your brought me my brother's children but you have brought me a knightess in shining armor. This is quite a surprise, and it certainly changes the situation. Remind me to give you a suitable reward."

Out of the corner of her eye, Carling caught Clank puff up his chest and smile.

The Commander began tapping his long scepter on the ground with one hand and tapping his cheek with the other, all the while looking at Carling. "So, it's true then," he finally said. "There is a silver breastplate. Now the question is: what do we do about it?"

The Commander returned to the dais, where he settled himself back down on his throne. The enormous

Centaur looked over the exhausted rag-tag group that filled his chambers. "Tradition has it that whomever wears the silver breastplate is the heir to the throne of Crystonia. You, my dear little Duende, cannot be allowed to continue wearing that breastplate. Clank, remove it."

Higson jumped in front of Carling. "Don't touch her," he said, glaring at Clank.

Two guards leaped forward and grabbed Higson while others held tightly to Tibbals and Tandum. Clank stepped up to Carling. "It would be my pleasure," he said, reaching toward her. The moment his fingers touched the silver breastplate, however, a loud crack like thunder filled the room and Clank fell backward, his four legs crumpling beneath him, as Carling's breastplate sent out a bright light and a high-pitched hum that filled the room.

The Centaurs raised their arms in an attempt to shield their eyes and ears.

When the noise and light dimmed, Carling dropped to her knees to check on Clank. He was not breathing, and his body was stiff and cold. The Centaurs around her began murmuring.

"She killed him!"

"We can't touch her."

"The breastplate is magical."

"She's possessed."

Suddenly, out of fear, the guards restraining Higson let him go. As soon as Carling realized he'd reached her side, she looked up at him, tears streaming down her cheeks. "I didn't mean to do that," she softly moaned. "I didn't know that would happen."

Higson wrapped his arms around his friend.

"I killed him," she sobbed.

171

"And he killed your parents," Higson said. "I'd say you got your revenge."

"But not this way. I never meant this way."

Their whispered conversation was interrupted by the Commander. "So, it appears our little lady has magical powers."

Carling looked up into his cold, cruel eyes that were nearly hidden by his silver brows. "I never meant to hurt anyone."

"So noble of you, I must say. This, however, calls for a change of strategy." The Commander stood in front of his throne and swished his long, black tail. "It is in my best interest to keep the existence of the breastplate, and its wearer, a secret from the races of Crystonia," he said, still addressing Carling. "I don't want it, or you, interfering with my plans to become the ruler of this great land. Therefore, I must keep you in my prison. If you go willingly, nothing will happen to your friends. If you do not, and I lose any more of my Centaurs, one by one, your friends will die."

CHAPTER 27

Miserable in Prison

CARLING FROWNED AS SHE considered the bleak circumstances in which she found herself. She had arrived in the cold dank cell hours before after winding down several steps and passing through one of those long dark corridors that cause an involuntary shudder to all who enter. Now, she sat on a stone bench designed for a Centaur that was so high off the dirt floor of her cell that her legs dangled in the air. No blanket or pillow had been provided to her. She could hear rain beating against the prison through the tiny slit of a window that provided her only source of fresh air and light. Exactly how long she had been in her cell she could not say. She had spent most of the time watching a thin ray of light from outside move across the floor.

She tried not to think of how roughly the guards had pulled Higson, Tibbals, and Tandum down the winding staircase and the long hallway lined with thick plank doors. One by one, she'd watched as each of her companions was shoved into a cell and the door was slammed shut and locked behind them. While Carling had been led to the last cell, far from her friends, no one had dared touch her.

Now, the tumor of terror that had started growing in the Commander's chambers completely filled Carling's entire being, pushing against her lungs and making it hard to breathe. Her body was weak from hunger and tired from the long journey. A vision of her burnt home appeared before her and she was overwhelmed with grief. Here she sat, alone in a dark, damp cell, her loyal friends also taken as prisoners, her parents dead. She had never wanted any of this.

She forced herself to push the dread deep inside. She was alive, after all, and her mind was still sharp and alert. She made a mental list of all the options she could think of, her first concern being for her friends. Unfortunately, the list was very short. She knew the Centaurs were all afraid to touch her as long as she was wearing the breastplate, but that didn't guarantee safety for Higson, Tibbals, and Tandum. As long as the Commander held her captive, she could not complete the task of collecting the stones and the war for the throne would continue, perhaps even escalate.

Her mind was a blur of activity, but none of her ideas seemed to rise to the top as being viable. She jumped down to the floor and started pacing in her narrow cell. As she neared the cell door, she heard someone whisper her name.

"Carling.... Carling.... Can you hear me?"

"Who is it?" she answered.

"It's Bale, the one with the burnt tail."

"Have you come to help me?"

"I don't know how...yet. But Dalt, the Centaur you rescued, has made it to the city. I thought you would want to know."

"Yes. That is good news. I hope he'll be alright."

"He will be, thanks to you. I brought you some food."

"My friends are in the first three cells in the hallway just as you turn the corner. Please give it to them."

"I have enough for all of you," Bale said, shoving a roll and some cheese through a narrow slot at the base of the door.

What could only be described as ecstasy flowed through Carling's body at the sight of the food. "Oh, Bale, thank you," she said. "Thank you so very much."

"You showed me mercy. I must find a way to repay it."

"You have. Believe me, you have!" she said, almost giggling. She had never been so grateful for food in her life. Of course, she had never gone without food for so long before, either.

Suddenly, Carling heard hoof beats outside her cell.

"I must go!" Bale whispered, fear evident in his voice. She heard him trot down the hall until his hoof beats mixed with those of others. She heard voices bouncing off the stone walls but couldn't make out what they were saying. She listened as the sound of the voices and the hooves on the stone floor got softer and softer until the sound of them disappeared altogether. She hoped Bale was safe and had been able to give food to her friends.

Slowly, she took a bite of the bread. The crust was thick and crunchy but the inside was soft and sweet. Next she took a bite of the cheese. It was a creamy white color, probably made from goats' milk. It nearly melted in her mouth. She couldn't remember ever eating anything so delicious. Even the bakers and cheesemakers in Duenton would have a hard time competing with this.

Her hunger satiated, she boosted herself up on her stone bench, lay down on her side, and immediately fell asleep. In her dreams, she was visited by the Wizard but he offered no words of advice or encouragement. He only sat beside her on the stone bench and stroked her auburn hair.

The heavy wooden door scraped across the dirt floor of her cell. "Wake up, sleeping beauty, the Commander wants to speak with you."

Carling rubbed her eyes and pushed herself up into a sitting position as she tried to focus. At first she didn't remember where she was. Then it all came rushing back and she felt her face flush and her heart pound. *The Commander! What could he want?*

She opened her mouth to speak but her mouth was so dry she couldn't form any words. She swallowed and her dry throat ached. Forcing the air out, she whispered, "May I have some water, please?"

"Water? Well, I suppose that's alright," the Centaur said as he pulled a leather pouch from the belt that cinched the black tunic tightly around his waist. Holding it above her mouth, he dripped some water in as a mother bird feeds its hatchling.

The drips of water dissolved quickly on her tongue but gave Carling the moisture she needed in order to speak. "What does the Commander want with me?"

"How would I know?" came the curt reply. "He doesn't consult with me before he does something, you know."

"No, I suppose not. I'm sorry."

"No skin off my haunches," the guard said, brushing aside her apology.

Carling followed him out the cell door, leaving it ajar. Another guard was waiting for them in the hallway outside her cell. He held a long spear in one hand. The Centaur who had entered her cell took the lead, Carling went next, and the other guard followed in the rear. They walked down the narrow, damp hallway, which was lit dimly by an occasional torch set into the wall. Carling recognized this as being the way they had come the previous day. Or was it the day before? She wasn't sure. When she was led around a corner, she recognized the three doors of the cells that held her companions. Suddenly, she cried out, "Higson, Tibbals, and Tandum!'

The guard whirled. "Do not speak!"

Sensing that he feared her and certain he would not touch her, Carling continued speaking to her friends. "Are you alright?"

"I said, do not speak!" the guard said, stomping a front hoof.

From behind each of the doors, a voice answered.

"I'm okay," said Higson.

"Hungry and thirsty but alive," said Tandum.

"I could really use a bubble bath and a brush," said Tibbals. Carling smiled at that.

The rear guard pounded his spear on the three doors. "Silence!"

"You don't need to behave like that," Carling said calmly. "They can't hurt you."

The guard snorted and jabbed her with the spear, tearing her tunic and cutting her upper arm. She stumbled against one of the doors with a cry of pain and slid to the floor.

"Carling! Carling! Are you alright?" shouted Higson from behind the door.

Carling reached up with one hand and covered the cut, but blood oozed out between her fingers. She glared up at the guard, who stood over her with a sneer on his face. "I'm fine," she said between clenched teeth.

"Get up! Get up, now," shouted the guard, poking her again with the spear but with less force this time.

Her arm throbbing, Carling gritted her teeth and struggled to her feet to the sounds of her friends yelling threats through their cell doors. She glared up at the Centaur who had stabbed her. "You could say you're sorry, you know."

He snorted. "I could but I won't. Now get moving!"

Carling followed the first guard up the same circular stairs they had come down the day before and, after many twists and turns, found herself outside the Commander's chambers. Two sentries opened the doors and motioned for Carling to enter.

Carling walked into the large, cold room, feeling very small but surprisingly confident. The Commander sat on his throne and watched as she crossed the mosaic pattern of the flagstone floor. His eyes glanced briefly at the blood that trickled down her arm, but he said nothing about it.

Carling's violet eyes found those of the Commander and she held his gaze as she walked directly up to the dais.

She stopped squarely in front of him. "You wanted to speak to me?"

The Commander smiled. "Yes, my dear. But I have found that the best conversations take place on a full stomach. Please join me, won't you?" Turning toward the servants who were stationed around the room, he added, "And would someone get something to clean up that arm. I detest the sight of blood."

Immediately, a mare approached Carling with a warm cloth and gently cleaned her cut, smiling sympathetically as she did so. Carling appreciated the show of kindness, something she had been sorely missing, and smiled back. Several other Centaurs appeared, carrying platters of food, the sight of which both thrilled and sickened her.

Standing in front of the copious amounts of food, Carling placed her hands on her hips and said, "I will not eat until my friends have been fed."

The Commander slowly smiled and nodded. "Very benevolent of you, I must say." Turning to his servants, he said, "Take some of this to the other prisoners." Immediately three Centaurs left the room with platters of food.

"Now, Knightess in Shining Armor, please eat."

Carling sat on a cushion that was placed on the floor, appreciating the softness, and took some fruit from the proffered tray. The sweet berries melted in her mouth and she ignored the juice that ran down her chin. She closed her eyes and took a moment to savor the sweetness, a stark contrast to the bitterness of her surroundings.

She continued to eat food from the trays that were offered to her until she was quite full. Only then did she look back up at the Commander, aware that his eyes had never left her.

She sucked in a deep breath. "So, why did you call me here? It certainly wasn't to make sure I was adequately fed."

The Commander chuckled. "You know, I actually find myself liking you, Knightess."

"My name is Carling."

He gave a wave of his hand and a slight bow of his head. "Alright then, *Carling*, let's get to the purpose of this meeting." The Commander's eyes sparkled dangerously and a cold smile lifted the corners of his mouth. "You are the wearer of the silver breastplate, a condition that it appears I can do nothing to alter, at least at this time. Yet you are tiny and weak. You need me and my army. It has occurred to me that we could make a great team, you and I. Together we could rule this land with an iron hoof."

"I prefer to rule with the four virtues the Wizard has instructed me to acquire," Carling replied.

"The Wizard? Tell me about this Wizard."

"The Wizard of Crystonia."

"I know nothing of such a Wizard."

"He is the one who gave me the breastplate and sent me on my quest to collect the four stones of light."

"I see only one stone."

"Yes," she said, her hand unconsciously covering the beautiful green stone. "It is the Stone of Mercy."

"Mercy?" he scoffed. "What good is that? You showed mercy to Clank and where did that get you? He turned around and brought you to me. On second thought, perhaps that was the best thing he could have done for you, bringing you to me, that is. Now, tell me about the other stones."

"I do not yet know about them. The Wizard is planning on my return to Duenton so he can give me further instructions."

"Well, no need of that. You don't need any more stones to make you powerful. I can provide all the power you need." He leaned forward, capturing her in his gaze. His eyes twinkled. "I have an army of hundreds of strong and well-trained warriors. As I initially proposed, let us band together. With you, the wearer of the silver breastplate, by my side, no one in Crystonia will question our right and authority to hold the throne. And if they should, my army will take care of them." The dangerous spark returned to the Commander's eyes as he looked down at her, awaiting her reply.

Carling felt her heart pounding in her chest. The palms of her hands felt wet and she wiped them on her pants legs, which were already quite soiled. She looked up at the Commander again. "I cannot take your offer. I must wait for instructions from the Wizard."

The Commander jumped to his hooves. "The Wizard!" he shouted. "I have heard quite enough about this worthless Wizard. What is he to us?" Motioning widely with his arms, he continued in a rant. "Does he have a castle? Does he have an army? No! All he has is a silly breastplate in need of completion. Ruling this land requires the strength of the Centaurs...the Heilodius Centaurs." He stopped and growled as he glowered down at Carling. "I only offered you this opportunity out of the goodness and generosity of my heart. Now I tire of you. Return to your cell, oh queen. I will not see you again unless you change your mind. Rot in the dungeon for the rest of your meaningless life for all I care!" He motioned for his guards to take her away before turning his back, his tail swishing in anger.

CHAPTER 28

Rescued

CARLING WAS RETURNED TO her cell, escorted by the same two guards. Once the door was slammed shut and the bolt slid loudly into place, everything around her became silent, both inside her cell and out. With only the dim morning sun casting a faint beam of light across the western stone wall, she was filled with a feeling of melancholy.

She sat on her stone slab, crossed her legs, rested her elbows on her knees, and held her chin in her hands. She needed to think. No, she needed to cry first...then perhaps she could think. For several minutes she let her fear and loneliness trickle down her cheeks. Finally, she opened her eyes, brushed away the remaining tears, and set her mind to thinking.

First she reviewed her audience with the Commander. Perhaps she had made a mistake and acted too hastily. Perhaps she could work with him and even control him. *No*, she decided. *There is no chance of that. His desire and objective had been to control me, not the other way around.* But if she worked with him, she could keep an eye on him. *No, what good would that do? He would surely do whatever he wanted anyway. Then again, perhaps that would be my only chance to free Higson, Tibbals, and Tandum.*

Her brain began to hurt as the battle went on within her head. How she wished her mother were here to help and advise her. It was so hard doing all of this alone. It was a lot to ask of a sixteen-year-old Duende with no worldly experience whatsoever. She felt her throat constrict and the backs of her violet eyes begin to sting as the tears threatened to return. She pursed her lips and took a deep breath, shook her head and brushed back her auburn hair.

She thought of the Wizard. Where was he now? Did he know about her captivity in Fort Heilodius? Did he know of the intentions of the Commander? If the answer to any of these questions was yes, why was he leaving her to face this alone? Couldn't he help?

She hopped off the stone slab and began pacing the length of her tiny cell. The day wore slowly on and her cell darkened even more with the setting of the sun. At last, she lay down on her rocky ledge that served as a bed and went to sleep.

A number of days passed. She knew this to be true because she'd been watching the thin strip of sunlight travel across her floor and finally disappear each day. Food and water were scarce. Both were slid through the slit in the base of the door at irregular intervals. She relished the water but the food was barely edible. No eating utensils were provided so she tipped the contents of each bowl into her mouth, trying not to look at what was inside and swallowing quickly. The muscles in her throat threatened to gag as what passed for food entered. She forced it down anyway, doing her best to avoid tasting it. Within an hour of each meal, Carling's stomach rebelled and she had to lie down to try to settle it.

Both the days and nights were equally quiet outside her cell door. She tried to call out to Higson, Tibbals, and Tandum, but the sound of her voice was absorbed by the moss-covered stone walls. She never heard a word from them. She tried not to let this worry her but it was hard not to feel uneasy. The Commander did not summon her again.

On the fifth or sixth, or maybe even seventh, day, Carling was sitting cross-legged on her stone bed, rehashing all that had transpired since she'd released an arrow toward a Centaur in a forest clearing. That event had proved to be the beginning of the end of the life she had once known. Now she was trapped inside a musty, dirty, stone cell. She felt the frustration rising inside her. She had to move. She unfolded her legs and hopped off the stone bench. She walked toward the slit that served as a window and pressed her face against the cold stone to get as close to the fresh air as she could. She took in a deep breath, closed her eyes, and exhaled slowly. Just as she did so, she heard her cell door open so quietly she could have easily missed the sound.

"Carling, follow me," she heard a voice say in a soft whisper.

Turning around quickly, Carling caught her breath. There, holding the door slightly ajar, was a short creature concealed by a black hooded cape. He tossed back the hood.

"Pik!" squealed Carling.

"Sh-h-h-h," said the Faun with his finger to his lips. "We must hurry, Missy."

"How did you find me?" she said as she ran to the door and resisted an urge throw her arms around him.

"A large eagle led me here. Follow me."

Carling realized immediately that the eagle was Baskus.

"But we can't leave without Higson, Tibbals, and Tandum," she said as she hurried toward the cell door.

"The other Fauns have them. Now quit talking and move!" He grabbed her hand and pulled her into the hallway.

They ran down the hall and turned the corner. Carling caught a glimpse of Tibbals' blond tail disappearing up the stairway. But her heart stopped when she saw a Centaur guard standing at the base of the stairs, letting them pass. He turned and motioned silently for them to come forward.

Carling hesitated but Pik moved boldly toward him. "It's okay. Come, Missy. Come with me," the Faun said.

When they reached the guard, he bent down and gave Carling a hug. "Hurry, little one. The sleeping potion I gave the guards won't last long."

"Bale! It's you," she exclaimed, a surge of excitement and gratitude flowing through her.

"And Dalt is up ahead. Now hurry," he said with a smile.

Carling and Pik quickly caught up with the rest of her companions. In the lead was another Centaur whom Carling assumed was Dalt. Even though he was limping on his left front leg, he was setting a fast pace down hallways and around corners. In one hand he carried a flaming torch that apparently had been removed from a wall sconce. The flames caused eerie bouncing shadows to slither and slink along the stone walls.

At each corner or intersection of passageways, Dalt stopped and then slowly, cautiously peeked around the corner. If all was clear, he waved them forward. They passed several guards who were sound asleep, snoring loudly. No one stopped them.

Finally, they went down a narrow passageway that ended at a wooden door that was so small the Centaurs would have to duck their entire upper bodies to get through. Dalt stopped in front of the door. He haltingly turned, his face grimacing. Carling could tell he was still suffering from his injuries and felt deep gratitude that he was taking such risks to help them.

"My friends," Dalt began, "this part of the Commander's citadel forms part of the wall surrounding the city. This door will lead you directly into the forest. You will need to work your way back to the east and south to get to your homes."

Pik stepped forward. "The Fauns have set up a camp downstream from the river that flows off the mountain. They are expecting you and will take care of you until we catch up."

Looking at Dalt, Carling asked, "Aren't you coming with us?"

"Oh, no. I would never make it. Plus, Bale and I can best serve you by delaying a search party that will surely be sent to find you. There will be quite an uproar as soon as your empty cells are discovered," he said with a smile.

Tibbals stepped up to Dalt, wrapped her arms around him and hugged him tightly. "We can't thank you enough."

His face flushed bright red as he returned the hug. "You saved my life. This was the least I could do to return the favor."

Releasing her, he looked down at Carling and Higson. "Go in peace, my little Duende. It is my hope that we will meet again under happier circumstances."

Carling pressed her lips together and blinked rapidly to hold back the tears. "Thank you, Dalt."

Bale stepped up and opened the little door. "Go quickly."

Tibbals and Tandum lowered their heads and torsos and scooted through the opening. Carling and Higson, being so short, didn't need to crouch. Pik and the other Fauns who had accompanied him came through last. Once outside, the Duende mounted their Centaurs and turned toward Bale and Dalt, who were bent low and peeking through the doorway.

"Goodbye, dear friends. May we meet again," was all Carling had time to say before Tibbals and Tandum set off in a gallop through the forest that clothed the sides of Mount Heilodius.

CHAPTER 29

Help from the Fauns

THE RIVER WAS QUITE easy to find. It flowed down the mountain from the glaciers at the peak of Mount Heilodius to the Swirling Sea on the east coast of Crystonia. The waterway's beating and crashing against the boulders was audible from quite a long distance. Tibbals and Tandum followed their ears and were soon drinking from the fresh cool snow melt. All the while, Carling kept glancing back to make sure they weren't being followed. They continued on by staying close to the river as Pik had instructed.

A few hours later, Carling sensed that they were not alone. At one point, she heard a branch snap. She jerked her head to the side and looked in the direction from which the sound had come. Nothing. Thinking it might have been just a forest animal, she didn't say anything to her companions.

A little further on, however, she was certain that she heard leaves rustling. "Stop, Tibbals," she whispered.

"What's the matter?" Tibbals asked, turning her upper body to look back at Carling.

"I keep thinking that I hear something."

"Like what?"

By this time, Tandum and Higson had stopped as well. When Carling voiced her concern, Higson tried to reassure her. "You've been in the forest enough to know there are lots of creatures moving around and making sounds," he said. "I'm sure there is nothing to worry about."

"I know. My nerves are frayed. I guess I'm just jumpy."

Tibbals patted her leg. "And you have every right to be after all we have been through."

"Let's keep moving," Tandum said as he started off, picking the easiest course he could find through the thick forest and fallen timbers.

They had traveled only a short distance when Carling heard another branch crack. "Stop! Something is out there, moving along with us. I'm sure of it."

Tibbals and Tandum stopped and looked from side to side, peering between the trees and under the ferns. "I see nothing, Carling," said Tandum.

"I know something or someone is following us. I can feel it."

"Then let him show himself," said Higson, puffing up his chest.

"But we have no weapons," said Tibbals. "The Heilodius took them, remember?"

"I have my hooves," said Tandum.

"You have nothing to fear," someone said. A Faun stepped out from behind a nearby tree.

Carling started, nearly falling off Tibbals. She calmed down as soon as she realized who it was. The Faun working his way through the underbrush toward them was one of the Fauns who had spent the stormy night in the cabin with them. One of Pik's companions.

"Are you the one who has been following us?" asked Carling.

"Yes. I didn't want to scare you. I was just sent to make sure you were safe. I'll lead you to the camp. Follow me."

The "camp," as the Faun called it, was no more than a small clearing encircled by a tight cluster of trees. Because the branches of the trees were so interwoven, the clearing was impossible to see from without. It had to be accessed by skirting a boulder and wading in the icy cold water of the mountain stream before climbing back up on the shore and squeezing between two trees and under branches. Carling and her friends would never have found it without help. No one else would, either. That was the idea.

Carling and her companions were welcomed warmly by the little group of runaway Fauns. The refugees struggling to get out from under the oppression of the Cyclops showed their gratitude to Carling with warm hugs and other expressions of affection. Now it was Carling who needed to express gratitude to the Fauns for the part they'd played in rescuing her from the clutches of the Commander.

Any celebrations were kept at a whisper, however, as they all had no idea if the Heilodius soldiers were tracking them. They ate what little food was available, mainly berries and bark, in near silence and by the light of the half-moon that peeked out from behind the rapidly moving clouds. Sleep came swiftly.

Sometime during the night, Carling awoke with a start. She heard shouts and complaints as a band of creatures splashed around in the mountain stream, not far from their hideout.

"How do you know this is the way they went?"

"I followed their tracks to the water's edge. But I can't find where they left the river."

"Perhaps they stayed in the water to cover their tracks."

"That could be. Let's continue downstream. But keep your eyes on the shore. This water is so cold, I doubt they would have stayed in it long."

The splashing and grumbling continued as the searchers, whom Carling assumed were Heilodius Centaurs, moved through the water...searching for them.

Her heart beat so loudly, she feared they would hear it. She held her breath. No one else in the little grove was moving. She had no idea how many of them were even awake, but it wouldn't surprise her if they all were.

Gradually, the voices and noise dimmed as the soldiers moved farther away. Apparently they had not found where Tibbals, Tandum, and their escort left the river. Perhaps they were protected by the darkness. Perhaps one of the Fauns had been wise enough to cover their tracks.

All was silent in the grove. Not a Centaur, Duende, or Faun moved until the searchers were gone.

"Is anyone else awake?" Tibbals whispered when the night stillness returned.

Seemingly everyone answered in the affirmative.

"Who was that?" the filly asked.

A Faun squeezed through the trees from the side by the river just in time to answer her question. "That was a group of ten Heilodius Centaurs. They were clearly looking for you. They must have discovered your empty cells."

"I hope Dalt and Bale are okay," Carling said, sitting up. "And has anyone seen Pik?"

"Pik arrived a while back and is on the lookout to the north," one of the Fauns answered.

At that moment, a Faun entered the clearing, struggling to catch his breath. It was Pik.

"Oh, Pik. I'm so glad you're safe," Carling whispered.

Gasping for breath, Pik responded. "I have been keeping an eye...huff, puff...on that bunch...huff...puff. They're good trackers, but they missed us. They're still moving..." Pik bent over, resting his hands on his hocks. "Huff...puff...downstream." He stood up and pressed his hands to his back. "They're...quite...huff, puff...a ways...huff, puff...away now."

Just before dawn the Fauns decided it was time to move on. They didn't want the Heilodius soldiers to come back in search of them in the light of day. They gathered what little possessions they had in their packs and started out with Pik in the lead. Carling and Higson mounted Tibbals and Tandum and followed.

"We might as well cross the river here, it's as good a place as any," Pik suggested. They all stepped off the bank and into the cold, rushing water.

Tibbals hesitated, remembering how cold the river was. Slowly, she lowered a long, elegant leg into the stream and shivered. Carling felt sorry for her and stroked her shoulder. By the time they were halfway across, the Fauns were swimming and Tibbals and Tandum were wading through water halfway up their flanks. Tibbals started trembling but kept moving. "Oh, what I wouldn't give for a hot bath and a soft bed right about now," she said.

Carling lowered her leg and dragged her toe in the water. She felt like sharing some of her friend's misery. The young Duende immediately understood what Tibbals was talking about. She clenched her jaw against the cold.

Just as they were crossing the deepest part of the river, Tibbals placed a front hoof on a loose rock. The rock tipped and the Centaur's hoof slipped to the side. Losing her balance, Tibbals went down into the river, taking Carling with her.

Carling gasped as she went under the surface, sucking in the icy cold water. As the river flowed over and around her, she felt herself tumbling. She quickly became disoriented and didn't know which way was up. Just as panic set in, she felt her body wedge against something solid. Suddenly, and none too soon, two hands grabbed her breastplate through her flapping tunic and pulled her out of the water. Coughing and choking, Carling was heaved up into the air. She opened her eyes and stared into those of Tandum. He had never looked so handsome!

"Are you alright, Carling?" Higson cried from where he sat perched tensely on Tandum's back.

She coughed and spit out water but nodded.

Tibbals was soon at her side. "Oh, Carling! I'm so sorry. Please forgive me."

Carling kept coughing up river water but waved her hand and shook her head in an effort to reassure Tibbals that no permanent damage had been done.

Pik left the shore and swam back to the little group in the middle of the river. "Everything okay here?" he asked, his face expressing concern.

"If I could stay on my hooves, everything would be fine," moaned Tibbals.

Carling caught her breath. "I'm okay, Tibbals. Are you?"

The filly's luxurious, long hair and tail hung in stringy, wet strands. "Yes," she said. "I love an ice cold bath. Let's get out of here!"

Tandum cradled Carling in his arms and carefully waded across the remainder of the river.

The Fauns hurried ahead, weaving through the woods in a southern direction. They spread out in an attempt to conceal their tracks and make it more difficult for the Heilodius Centaurs to follow them. Pik stayed close beside Tandum and Tibbals.

Tibbals was limping slightly. She had pulled a ligament in her foreleg when she slipped. As a result, Carling sat upon Tandum, right behind Higson, her arms wrapped tightly around him. The smile on the young Duende's face indicated that he didn't mind one bit.

By mid-day, the travelers were weary. But they kept moving forward, spurred on by the fear that the Heilodius Centaurs might be following them. They had no idea where the soldiers might be and could only wish the Centaurs had returned to Fort Heilodius, though no one in the group thought this was likely.

Just when the travelers decided to pause and rest, the two Fauns who had been traveling in the front turned back around. Facing the group, they held up their hands for silence.

"There is something going on ahead," said one.

"We don't know what, so we are going to investigate," said the other. "All of you stay here and lie low."

Carling looked around Higson's shoulder. She felt her pulse quicken. Tandum folded his front legs and lowered his body to the ground. Tibbals did the same. Carling and Higson climbed off Tandum's back. All of the Fauns sat themselves on the ground, backs to the center of a circle, and peered into the forest around them.

It wasn't long before the two advanced scouts returned. Gasping for breath, they made their report.

"There is a battle going on in the meadow just beyond the edge of the forest," said one.

"The Centaurs that were looking for us are fighting a band of Cyclops," added the other. "It looks like the Cyclops have them greatly outnumbered."

Pik stepped forward. "I suggest we go to the edge of the forest, where we can keep an eye on things. I don't want to be surprised by just sitting here and waiting."

Tandum spoke up. "Do you think it's wise for us all to go? Perhaps I could go with a couple of you and keep an eye on things. I can return quickly if need be."

Pik glanced at Tandum. "That is a generous offer, but I would prefer that we remain together. We will stay concealed in the trees."

It was decided and the group moved out. Soon they heard the clamors and clashes of the battle. They hurried forward and secreted themselves behind trees and bushes at the edge of the meadow. Each of them had a clear view of the gruesome battle taking place in what would otherwise have been a beautiful, peaceful flower-filled field.

The Centaurs were experts with the bow and arrow. The weapon of choice for the Cyclops, however, was the

Khopesh, also called the sickle-sword. A deadly cross between a sword and a battle ax, it was made from a single piece of bronze and was very heavy. But the Cyclops were big, strong beasts, so wielding their Khopeshes was no problem for them.

The Centaurs' arrows, which were designed for fighting from a distance, were perfect for the speed and agility that their four legs afforded them. The Cyclops' Khopeshes needed to be used close up to their targets, so the Cyclops had to do a lot of running to reach their enemy.

The Cyclops also made a lot of noise during battle. Their shouts and growls were constant and served to inspire and encourage one another. The Centaurs were much quieter as they galloped around the perimeter of the circle of Cyclops. Other than the pounding of their hooves, they only made sounds when struck, at which point they emitted blood-curdling cries of pain.

Carling watched with a mixture of fear and disgust. She abhorred violence, and this was violence of the worst kind. "Can't we do something to stop this?" she whispered to Higson.

Tandum, hearing her, said, "There is nothing we can do. We are too few in number and unarmed at that. The battle will simply have to play itself out, and the strongest will be the victor."

Higson patted Carling's leg. "They have chosen this. Perhaps the quest we are on will put an end to such violence, once and for all."

"Let us only hope," added Tibbals.

"I fear there will be much more bloodshed before a queen rules the land," answered Tandum prophetically.

CHAPTER 30

The Battlefield

THE BATTLE CARRIED ON into the night. Carling and her companions stayed hidden behind the trees, watching the whole encounter. Carling felt riveted to her spot, fear and foreboding keeping her frozen in place behind a pine tree. She was exhausted to the bone, but she didn't dare sleep. Looking from side to side, she saw that her companions, too, were awake and keeping their eyes on the battle.

At some point, a few torches were lit. By whom, Carling couldn't have said. The torches provided an eerie sort of light and cast giant shadows around the meadow, shadows that danced across and between the trees. From Carling's vantage point at the edge of the forest, it was clear that the Cyclops were winning the clash. Several of each race now lay dead or dying around the meadow but, since the band of Cyclops greatly outnumbered the Centaurs, there were still plenty of them left to carry on the battle.

Just before dawn, the fighting abruptly ended. The two Heilodius Centaurs that were still able to gallop on four legs disappeared into the forest just to the west of where Carling was hiding. The Cyclops lowered their Khopeshes and watched them go, deep growls emanating from their chests. Without taking the time to check on their fallen comrades, the Cyclops lumbered off, moving to the south, away from where Carling, Higson, Tibbals, Tandum, and the Fauns were hiding.

The rising sun ignited the western sky with splashes of pink and gold. The contrast between the beauty of the sunrise and the horror of the battlefield sickened Carling. She reached over and clutched Higson's hand. He put his arm around her and hugged her tightly. When her nerves and stomach had settled, a new resolve filled her. "Let's go help them," she said, motioning with her chin toward the fallen Centaurs and Cyclops, some of whom were still alive and moaning in agony. Higson knew better than to argue.

Carling took the lead, instructing her troops to spread out over the battlefield to see who could be helped. Many were dead. But there were several who simply needed their injuries treated and bleeding stopped. Soon, clothing was being ripped into strips to make bandages. Some of the Fauns took the job of shuttling water from a nearby stream to quench dry throats and clean wounds.

Carling set to work on a large, very smelly Cyclops. She had never been near one before, having only seen the one band from a distance as they traveled to Manyon Canyon. She felt herself shiver as she knelt beside him. He lay on his back and moaned pitifully. His hairy arms and legs were matted with blood, and she really wasn't sure where to begin.

"What can I do to help you?' she asked.

Without opening his eyes, he whispered through cracked and parched lips, "Water."

Carling looked around until she located one of the Fauns that had been sent to fetch water. "Over here!" she shouted.

The Faun came running to her with a flagon of water. Holding it over the Cyclops' mouth, he let the water drip. The Cyclops opened his large eye and began lapping at the water like a dog. Carling watched, her heart aching with sympathy. When the Cyclops drank as much as he wanted, he dropped his large, horned head back to the ground and closed his eye. He began moaning again. Carling and the Faun used the rest of the water to clean his wounds. Carling took her cape, the only garment she had left other than her tunic, and tore it into strips. She wrapped the Cyclops' arms and legs tightly to stop the bleeding. Then she gently patted him on the shoulder and moved on to the next injured and barely living warrior.

A Centaur was lying crumpled up not far away from where she had been working on the Cyclops. Carling moved to his side. He turned his face and Carling jerked back, her hand unconsciously moving up to cover the cut on her arm. This was the same Centaur who had stabbed her with the spear in the Commander's prison. The wound she bore on her arm was still far from healed.

"So," he said in a pain-laden whisper, "you recognize me."

Carling nodded.

"Then pass me by."

Carling slowly shook her head. "What can I do to help you?"

Surprise flashed briefly in his eyes, followed by suspicion. "You would help me? Why?"

"You're suffering."

He nodded. "That is true." He sucked in as much breath as his lungs would hold before adding in a soft, raspy voice, "There is nothing you can do. It is too late for me. Move on to someone else."

"Don't talk. You're too weak. I will clean and dress your wounds." A Faun brought water and Carling tore up more of her cape. She did her best to bind the Centaur's wounds. Many thoughts filled her head as she worked, most of them centered around the Stone of Mercy that she wore on her chest. While her arm still bore the wound from this Centaur's mistreatment, it surprised her that her heart carried no animosity toward him. It occurred to her that mercy must be born of forgiveness, or perhaps the other way around. She wasn't sure how this all happened, only that it did and it was powerful.

As Carling worked, the Centaur watched her, his eyes expressing the questions in his heart. When she got up to leave, he reached up for her hand. "I'm sorry that I hurt you," he whispered.

Carling squeezed his hand, smiled down at him, and moved on to the next injured warrior.

CHAPTER 31

Journey Home

AFTER SEVERAL HOURS OF providing what medical attention Carling and her friends were able to give, they checked one last time on their patients and decided to continue on their journey to the village of Duenton. They still had a long way to go and knew they would be lucky to reach their destination by sunset the following day.

The experience of watching the brutal battle and attempting to heal the suffering warriors had taken its toll on Carling. She felt both weak and exhausted. She found herself drifting to sleep on the back of Tandum, clutching tightly to Higson. During her waking moments, Carling kept thinking about the power struggle in which she was immersed. Carling was to become the ruler of this entire land. It was a bittersweet realization, for the cost had been the loss of her home and family and everything she had ever known. She was returning to her village, but for how long? She knew the Wizard would send her on another quest to retrieve a second stone, but when?

The night was uneventful, for which Carling was grateful. Hunger and exhaustion were taking their toll on everyone, so it was good to at least get some rest. The morning dawned with a light cloud cover but no rain, which provided additional relief. They moved out quite early.

Tibbals' fetlock, which had been injured during the fall in the river, felt much better after a good night's rest. "Carling, I'm not limping today," she said. "You can ride me."

"Are you sure that's wise?"

"Oh, sure. If it starts to hurt, I'll tell you and you can go back to Tandum."

Carling looked over at Higson. He had a frown of disappointment on his face, and Carling realized he had enjoyed having her arms around him. She smiled to herself as she climbed up on the filly's back.

They traveled toward Mount Dashmoore, which was visible on the southeastern horizon. They were grateful they could see it now and let it serve as their guide toward their destination...home. The knowledge that the City of Minsheen rested on the mountain's southern slopes and the village of Duenton lay just beyond that provided encouragement. They also appreciated the cloud cover that shielded their eyes from the glare of the sun. No one said much as they traveled along, apparently lost in their own thoughts.

When they stopped by a stream for a mid-day break, Pik ran up to them. "Everyone doing okay?" he asked.

"We are," responded Tandum.

"Carling," the Faun said, looking up at the beautiful Duende to where she sat mounted on the filly's back.

"Yes, Pik?" she said.

"All of the Fauns are concerned about how well we will be received by your village. We have decided to stop a ways back and let you go on with Tibbals and Tandum. You can discuss our presence with the village leaders and find out if we would be welcome. Then return to us and report."

Carling nodded and bit her lip. She wondered if she was ready to approach the elders of the village. To them, she was just a young girl... a girl who had caused her village a lot of trouble. She regretted that she was not more prepared for this.

Higson patted her hand. "Don't worry, Carling. You'll do fine."

She smiled weakly. She wished she had even a tiny amount of confidence in herself. "I hope so," she responded.

Tibbals joined in. "Don't ever forget who you are! You are the future queen of Crystonia. You have already displayed amazing courage and leadership just in the few weeks we've been gone." Tibbals paused and looked over at her brother, then added, "And if you'll have us, we'll stay by your side through whatever comes along. Right, Tandum?"

Tandum looked askance. "Whatever?"

Tibbals giggled. "Yes, big brother. Whatever!"

As they moved across the plain, each member of the company kept glancing up at Mount Dashmoore. Carling wished the mountain would come to them instead of them having to trudge all the way to it. Near the end of the day, they entered the forest that surrounded the base of the mountain, causing them to lose sight of the landmark for which they were aiming.

To Carling, the forest provided a welcome indication that she was almost home. She had always loved her excursions with Higson into the western edge of this very forest. She felt a renewal of energy flow through her body. "We're almost there," she said to Tibbals.

"Thank goodness. I don't know how much more of this my hooves can take without getting a pedicure."

Carling giggled and reached up to plait Tibbals long blond hair into a pretty braid. She had become quite an adept Centaur rider and could keep her balance without holding on.

By late afternoon, they reached the peak of the ridge of foothills that bordered the western edge of their valley. The Duende called this long series of hills with a narrow crest and steep slopes on both sides a hogback. The climb up to the peak of the ridge had been strenuous so, once they reached the top, all were happy to take a break.

Carling looked to the east. She had never been up to the top of the hogback. Now she stood looking down at her village with a mixture of joy and sadness. Joy at finally returning. It felt like she had been gone much longer than a few weeks. So much had happened. She was no longer the same girl who had left in search of the Stone of Mercy. Perhaps it was the stone that had changed her.

The sadness was brought on by the loss of her parents. Other than Higson's parents, no one in that village upon which she now gazed was awaiting her return. Perhaps no one was even aware she had left. She felt a longing so intense it made her insides hurt. How desperately she ached to have her mother's arms around her again.

She wrapped her own arms around her body and hugged herself tightly. She felt the silver breastplate and for a moment wished she had never found it. The little Duende took a deep breath and pursed her lips. She looked from side to side at the friends who surrounded her. Other than good old Higson, they were all new, yet she realized that she loved them. While no one could replace her parents, these new friends had managed to fill part of the hole in her heart. Her mouth turned up in a silent smile and tears moistened her violet eyes. I will be grateful, she told herself.

Just as the sun was setting, the weary travelers arrived in the very meadow where Carling first saw the event that had set all of this in motion. At least that was how she viewed it. She did not know that everything had really started before her birth, when the Wizard of Crystonia paid visits to the smithy Ashtic and to Carling's mother.

The Fauns stopped. "We will settle in here for the night," Pik said.

Carling could tell Tibbals was eager to return home. Her dainty prancing told her as much. "We will keep moving," Carling said. "Tibbals and Tandum will take us to Duenton, then return to their home in the City of Minsheen. Higson and I will meet with the village elders tomorrow, then come to you after we have an answer."

Thus the plan was set and Tibbals and Tandum, with their Duende friends on their backs, took off through the forest at a canter.

CHAPTER 32

The Council of Elders

CARLING WAS CONTENT TO remain in that happy state, floating somewhere between asleep and awake. She was warm and comfortable and her stomach was full. She hadn't felt that way for weeks. Perhaps all of these facts played a part in helping her sleep so soundly once sleep overcame her. Even her dreams had not frightened and awakened her. With regret, she slowly opened her eyes and looked around. She recognized Higson's family home at once.

Sunlight was streaming in the little round window set high on the southern wall. Tree limbs from outside cut the rays of light into irregular ribbons. She breathed in the smell of something wonderful being baked in the kitchen, one of Higson's mother's famous creations, no doubt.

Their greeting the previous night had been joyous. Higson's mother couldn't stop crying and hugging each of them. His father wanted a day-by-day account of what had transpired since their departure, a request that neither Carling nor Higson had the energy to fulfill.

Carling stretched her arms over her head, threw back the covers, and swung her feet out and down to the floor. She went to the mirror, the same mirror she had checked before she started on her quest to find the Stone of Mercy. She was surprised that she still looked the same. Somewhere deep in the back of her mind, she had assumed that she would look different. She knew that on the inside she was different, and it seemed only right that it would show in her outward appearance. But no. Staring back at her was the same, youthful Duende face she was accustomed to. The same violet eyes that captivated others. The same thick, auburn hair forming a halo around her face. The same short, pixie nose. The same high cheekbones. The same thin lips. All fitting together to form a beautiful face. *Something about that face should have changed,* she thought.

She washed up and brushed her thick hair, then put on the silver breastplate and covered it with a clean tunic.

She felt her heart skip a beat as her thoughts turned to the commission for the day. She wished she had something more attractive than just a plain, old tunic to wear. She took a deep breath, lifted her chin, and walked out the bedroom door.

The town elders worked in a large stone building at the north end of the town square. Thankfully, the building had not been damaged when the Heilodius Centaurs attacked. Perhaps they had viewed it as too difficult to bother with and spent their time, instead, on easier targets. Whatever the reason, it stood out as an imposing structure...something to be reckoned with, to be sure.

Carling and Higson slowly ascended the long stone staircase. To Carling, it wasn't long enough. The two impressive and intricately carved wooden doors at the top stood firmly shut. The two little Duende stopped in front of them and gazed up, the doors towering over them. Carling wondered why they needed such tall doors. Higson reached up to open one of them, but Carling grabbed his hand.

Higson looked over at her. "Are you okay?"

"I just need a minute to catch my breath," she answered.

Higson waited patiently.

After a few minutes, Carling withdrew her hand and nodded. "Okay. Let's go."

"You can do this, Carling."

"I hope so."

With much effort, Higson opened the enormous door. They stepped into a large, square vestibule. The floor was decorated with sparkling stone tiles. Overhead, hanging down from a very high ceiling, a sparkling chandelier holding dozens of candles lit the room. The walls were painted with murals depicting Duende at work. Multiple doors just off the foyer were currently closed. A few gilded chairs rested against the walls. Carling had never seen such opulence in the village of Duenton. She was surprised. Yes, the Duende were artisans and certainly had the skills to create such magnificence, but they were also a very hard-working and practical people. Their homes, before the attack, that is, had been on the simple side. Carling never imagined the town leaders had surrounded themselves with such excessive grandeur.

At the far end of the room was a set of double doors that were nearly as tall as the ones through which they had just come. In front of these doors, an older Duende woman sat at an ornately carved desk. The woman was looking down and writing something with a quill pen. The plume bounced around as she worked. She either hadn't noticed their arrival or didn't care; Carling couldn't tell which.

Carling looked over at Higson. He winked at her, took her hand, and led her forward. They stopped in front of the desk. The woman still did not look up.

"Good Morning, ma'am," Higson said politely.

"What do you want?" she responded brusquely, finally lifting her eyes and looking over the top of her spectacles.

"We would like an audience with the town council," Carling said, trying to sound confident and professional, though she felt far from it.

The woman shook her head. "I'm so sorry, children, but that is impossible. They are in their daily council meeting." She motioned her head toward the closed doors behind her, then looked back down and continued with her writing.

"We have something very important to discuss with them," Carling continued.

The woman slapped down her pen in irritation. "I'm sure you do. Everyone does. But I cannot interrupt their meeting."

"Oh, I think you can."

Carling and Higson started. The deep, mellow voice came from behind and above them. Carling recognized it immediately. She turned around quickly and gazed up at Vidente, the Wizard of Crystonia. It suddenly occurred to her why the doors needed to be so tall.

The Wizard's hood was off his head and draped over his shoulders. His face was now clearly visible. He looked much younger than Carling had imagined he would be. The only wrinkles on his face were smile wrinkles at the sides of his blue eyes, eyes which sparkled beneath bushy eyebrows. His beard was brown and trimmed neatly. His cheeks were pronounced yet, at the same time, round and rosy. She cocked her head to one side and examined him closely. She was sure that he had a long gray beard when she last saw him.

"Wizard," she said. She felt herself relax, not having realized until now just how tense she had been. "You're here."

He smiled down at her, causing the wrinkles near his eyes to deepen. "Yes, Carling. I thought you might need some help."

Carling wanted to run to him and hug his legs, but she kept control of her impulse. Instead she simply said, "Yes. I really would appreciate that. But...." she paused.

Vidente asked, "What is it?"

"I thought you had a gray beard."

Vidente chuckled. "I decided to change it up a bit. What do you think?"

Carling nodded. "It's nice. Makes you look younger."

"Well that's a good thing, don't you think?"

"Perhaps."

"Perhaps?" he answered.

"Well, the other one made you look..."

"Wiser?" he added with a smile.

Carling wrinkled her nose and grinned. "Yes...sort of."

Vidente laughed and patted Carling on the head.

Awed by the sudden appearance of the Wizard, the Duende woman behind the desk scrambled to her feet. "J-j-just a moment. I-I-I'll be right back." She dashed through the doors and into the council room, returning a moment later with two of the village elders, one male and one female.

The elders walked into the vestibule and around the desk, approaching the Wizard with a noticeable amount of trepidation. "Welcome, oh venerable Wizard. To what do we, the humble creatures of Duenton, owe a visit from your greatness?"

Vidente held up one hand, the red ring on his middle finger glistening brightly. "Perhaps you know these two young Duende from your village?" he said, motioning to Carling and Higson.

The elders glanced at the two of them. "It is true that we do know them," said the woman.

"What trouble have they gotten themselves...and all of us...into now?" said the male elder.

"Into trouble, you ask? Ah-h-h. You misunderstand them." Turning toward Carling, the Wizard said, "I think it is time that you show them the silver breastplate, Carling."

Carling pulled back her cape and unwrapped her tunic, revealing the silver breastplate.

The woman gasped. The man stiffened. "I think you had better come into the council chambers," he said.

The Duende woman behind the desk scurried back and opened both doors as wide as they would go. Vidente entered the room ahead of them all, moving as if floating on air. Carling and Higson went through the doorway next, followed by the village elders.

The room they entered, which was even more elegant than the entrance hall, smelled of the sweet perfume of flowers. Large fluted columns lined the walls and supported the high ceiling. The walls were painted a pale blue and covered with ornate tapestries depicting Duende at play...something Carling could never remember seeing the industrious little race do in real life. Between the tapestries, tall stained glass windows let the sunlight fill the room with color and dance along the floor, which was a continuation of the mosaic design in the outer hall. The entire chamber was clearly a testament to the artistry of the Duende builders who had created it. It was breathtakingly beautiful.

Once they were all inside the room, the doors were shut behind them. Carling stopped behind Vidente, but took a moment to peek around his long gray cloak. In the front of the large room was a semi-circle of six tables. Two Duende sat at each table, making twelve council members in all. To a teenager like Carling, they all looked very old. The two elders who had come out to meet them stepped forward and took their places in the empty chairs in the middle.

Vidente introduced himself. "My esteemed body of elders. I am Vidente, the Wizard assigned to oversee the affairs of Crystonia." He paused and looked each elder in the eyes. Some smiled under his scrutiny. Others squirmed.

The woman who had come out to meet them initially spoke up first. "I am Shanta, the president of the Council of Elders. We welcome you to the village of Duenton, Vidente. We are your humble servants."

"No, ma'am. It is I who have come to serve you," he said with a kind smile. "Let me get right to the purpose of my visit. There is a war in the land that has been going on for hundreds of years. You, in your little valley, have been spared from exposure until recently. You were not considered a threat to those seeking power. But all that has changed. From this day forward, the little visitation by the Heilodius herd vandals...."

"Little?" interrupted one of the more skeptical of the elders.

Vidente turned and looked deeply into his eyes. "Yes...little. You have no idea to what ends the other races will go to secure the throne on Mount Heilodius. The damage that was done to your village was little compared to what war is capable of once it reaches your home."

All of the elders began fidgeting in their seats. They looked back and forth at one another.

One spoke up. "Why must we be involved in this power struggle? What has changed that involves us?"

Shanta answered for the Wizard. "Bring forth the girl."

Carling, who had watched the introduction from behind the safety of the Wizard's robe, swallowed hard. She suddenly felt very thirsty. She looked over at Higson, who nodded at her and smiled by way of encouragement. She took a deep breath and stepped up beside the Wizard. Shivering, she looked up at him as he towered over her. Carling felt very small, but his kind eyes warmed and uplifted her.

"Carling, show the council what you are wearing," the woman said. Then she caught her breath and looked up at the Wizard. "Forgive me. Is it alright if she reveals the breastplate to the others?"

Vidente gave them a brief nod of his bearded chin.

Once again, Carling pushed aside her cape and unwrapped her tunic. This time, her fingers were trembling.

The elders let out a collective gasp, just as Shanta and her partner had upon seeing the breastplate in the foyer.

"What does this mean?" said one.

"Is it truly the silver breastplate of the ruler of Crystonia?" asked another.

"Where did she get that?" queried a third.

"Wizard, please explain what is going on," said the man who sat beside Shanta.

The Wizard dipped his head and looked down at Carling. Placing a hand gently on her head, he whispered to her. "Let it begin, my Carling. Let it begin." He looked back up at the council. "I will let Carling explain."

Carling placed the palms of her hands against the breastplate. "Dear Village Elders. I understand your shock at seeing this breastplate on me. I assure you, no one is more surprised than I that I possess it. I, too, have grown up hearing the stories of the silver breastplate. I had always been told that the wearer of it would be the rightful heir to the throne that sits empty on Mount Heilodius. I never aspired to be that person. When the Wizard of Crystonia first visited me, I felt sure he had made a mistake. I'm still not convinced that he hasn't. However, I have committed myself to fulfill the assignments he gives me to prepare for this responsibility." She paused and brushed a few tendrils of her auburn hair off her forehead and tucked them behind her right pointed ear. She was surprised at how relaxed she felt. The tension and, yes, fear that had filled her before were gone. She placed her fingertips together, forming a steeple, then pressed them against her lips as she thought about what she should say next.

"I have just returned from my first assignment...to secure the Stone of Mercy." All eyes in the room, except hers and the Wizard's, glanced down at the sparking green stone on the breastplate. "I have learned on this quest that what the Wizard says is true. There is a fierce battle going on all around us. It will soon enter our valley and we must be prepared."

One of the elders cleared his throat and growled. "Then it is you that will bring this war to our doorstep."

Vidente spoke up. "When word gets out that the wearer of the silver breastplate is in your midst, you will, indeed, become a target. That is why we must begin preparations now to protect you."

"Perhaps the wiser course would be for young Carling to simply leave," suggested another.

Carling felt a stab of pain pierce her heart.

"That is a short-sighted approach," answered the Wizard. "Regardless of whether she is here or not, the Duende will become a target of the greed and power struggle that is going on."

"We never asked for this," said Shanta. "We are a peace-loving people. We never hurt anyone. We simply go about our business."

The Wizard nodded. "That is true. But that is in the past and of no relevance now. Carling has been chosen to become the future queen of Crystonia. You cannot hide from that. You must prepare yourselves for what is to come."

Carling clenched her jaw and boldly stepped forward. "I have a plan."

CHAPTER 33

Carling's Plan

IMMEDIATELY, CARLING HAD EVERYONE'S rapt attention. "In the meadow at the base of the hogback," she said, "there are twelve Fauns awaiting my return. They are refugees from the Cyclops. They saved my life and I promised them sanctuary among the Duende."

"You what?" one of the elders nearly shouted. He was silenced immediately by Vidente's raised hand.

"Yes," Carling continued. "I promised that we would shelter them. Now I realize that we need them as much as they need us."

"H-how could we possibly need the likes of them?" sputtered another of the elders.

"They are bigger and stronger than we are. They are good workers, and my plan to secure our village will require their assistance."

"And just what is your plan?" inquired Shanta, not unkindly.

"I would like us to build a wall around the entire village." Carling pulled a rolled-up piece of parchment out of the bag that was looped over her shoulder. "May I approach?" she asked.

Shanta nodded.

Carling and Higson walked up to the center table. Vidente remained where he stood as a smile, half-hidden by his beard, played across his face.

Carling and Higson opened the roll and smoothed it out. As Carling began explaining, the other elders moved around so they could see as well. "I envision a high earthen bank around the entire village," Carling explained. "On the top of the embankment, we would insert vertical tree trunks whose tops have been sharpened to a point. We will have only one entrance, on the west," she moved her hand and pointed her delicate finger at a marking on the west side of the village. "You can see that here," she said, tapping the paper.

She paused for a moment, trying to decide what else to tell them. "Oh, yes. Here, here, here, and here," she said, pointing at different places on the diagram, "we will build watch towers. The Fauns can actually help us man these towers as well as help us build the embankment."

One of the elders straightened. "You are proposing that we live in a fort?"

"Of sorts, yes."

"Do you really think this is necessary?" asked another.

The Wizard stepped forward at last. "What Carling proposes is not only necessary, it is essential for your survival. And let me stress one more thing: it is of the utmost urgency that you begin to build this immediately."

CHAPTER 34

Attack on the Fauns

WHEN CARLING AND HIGSON returned to Higson's family cottage, they found Tibbals and Tandum waiting for them. Tandum looked freshly groomed and very handsome. But Tibbals was breathtaking. Her golden body sparkled. She wore a beautiful pink tunic with a bejeweled belt around her waist. Her long blond hair and tail were clean and braided with ribbons and flowers. Her hooves and fingernails were freshly painted with pink glitter.

"Oh, Tibbals, you look so beautiful!" exclaimed Carling.

Tibbals twirled around, smiling and giggling. Carling realized she had missed those giggles during their journey. "It feels so good to be clean again," the filly said. "I'm not sure forests and battlefields are the places I was meant to dwell in!"

Carling laughed. "Nor any of us!" A twinge of guilt spread through her body. Dare she ever ask Tibbals to accompany her on another quest assigned to her by the Wizard? She fingered the empty holes in her breastplate and her body quivered. When would that happen? She had no idea but sensed it would be soon. For the moment, they had a monumental task to perform to protect her village.

"And look at you, Carling. You are absolutely glowing," Tibbals said, scooping up her little friend and giving her a hug. Carling smiled as she was pulled out of her reverie.

"It appears the meeting with the village elders went well," Tandum stated.

"Carling was amazing," said Higson.

"Not me. It was the Wizard. Without him, I doubt we could have even gotten in the chambers."

"The Wizard was there?" asked Tibbals.

"How did he even know you were going?" responded Tandum.

Carling shook her head, wonderment filling her eyes. "I don't know how he knows what he knows or does what he does. But he was there and the elders listened to everything we said."

"And the Fauns? What of the Fauns?" asked Tibbals.

"Let's go pay them a visit right now," said Carling, excited by the communal energy her friends provided.

Tibbals and Tandum carried Carling and Higson back through the forest on the same path they had traveled just a day before. When they reached the meadow, they found the Fauns still sleeping, scattered across the ground like rubble after a windstorm. Carling almost felt guilty disturbing them, but the sense of urgency that had filled her in the council chambers was still strong within her.

She leaped off Tibbals and ran up to the first crumpled body of a Faun. She reached down and shook him. As she did so, he groaned and rolled onto his back. Carling gasped and jumped back. The face staring up at her belonged to Pik, but it looked more dead than alive. His eyes were sunken and glassy. His cheeks were splotchy. His lips were cracked and blackened.

Carling quickly got a hold of herself and bent over her friend. "Pik, what happened? What went on here?"

"Poison," he whispered.

Carling bent closer to his mouth. "What? Tell me again."

Pik took a breath and shuddered as he let it out. "Our water. Poison."

Higson hurried over to Carling's side and knelt beside her. "What happened?" he said, panic evident in his voice.

"He said something about poison."

"Chancy went to fetch water yesterday," Pik forced out. "A stranger," he paused to cough violently. "A stranger," he began again, "gave him water. It must have been poisoned."

Carling sat back on her heels, her eyes wide with horror. She looked at Higson.

Higson clenched his jaw. "Who could have done this? Who was that stranger?"

"I don't know," Carling said, "but we must help them, and fast."

She and Higson helped Pik onto Tibbals' back. Higson climbed on Tandum, and the two centaurs hurried, as quickly as they dared, back to the village. While Higson informed the villagers that a dozen very sick Fauns were coming and recruited everyone to help, Tandum and Tibbals galloped back to retrieve two more Fauns.

While they were gone, Carling went from Faun to Faun to determine which ones needed the most help. Her heart sank as she realized they all looked bad. All seemed on the verge of death.

She looked around her. "Wizard! Wizard, where are you? Can you come help me?" she pleaded at the top of her voice.

Silence.

She called out again. "Vidente, please hear my petition. I need your help."

Silence again. The Wizard did not appear. Carling remained alone in the meadow with the dying Fauns.

As soon as Tibbals and Tandum returned, Carling helped two Fauns onto the backs of the Centaurs. "Can you hold on?" she asked, clearly concerned. They both nodded weakly as they slumped against the Centaurs' backs. Two by two, Tibbals and Tandum carried all the Fauns to the village.

The Duende in the village scurried around, trying to help. The village healer, a very old woman named Cantessa, rushed to her home and began mixing a potion. However, not knowing what the poison was that the Fauns had consumed, she was just making her best guess. Her most significant clue was the black lips. That hinted at the plant found on the slopes of the hogback that the villagers called Nightspell. It was a lovely purple flower but, when crushed, it secreted a tasteless, odorless substance that dissolves in water. It is very poisonous to some creatures, though, strangely, not to all. Those affected by it displayed the telltale sign of the black lips and tongue. If Nightspell had been in their water, and the Fauns were affected by it, she knew she needed to act quickly. Once the blackness appeared on the lips and tongue, it would soon spread to the heart. A blackened heart would stop beating.

Cantessa dashed to her cupboards and threw open the doors. Brushing aside cobwebs, she searched through a series of dusty bottles, pulling out one after another. When her counter was covered with bottles of different shapes and sizes, she began mixing and stirring with such vigor that the orange liquid she was creating splashed on her yellow blouse. Paying no attention, she rushed out of her cottage, spoon and bowl in hand.

As each Faun arrived, he was bedded down in the foyer of the very government building where Carling had, only hours before, arrived feeling such trepidation. Cantessa dashed up the steps, splashing still more of her potion on her clothing. The Duende at the entrance opened the tall doors and let her enter. The village healer went from one Faun to the next, forcing them to drink a large spoonful of the foul-smelling and bitter-tasting concoction. Then she stepped back, watched, and waited.

Carling entered the antechamber, perspiration beading on her forehead. She had ridden Tibbals as Tandum carried the last Faun to the village. Now she walked beside the weak creature, holding his limp hand, as several Duende helped get him down from Tandum's back. They carried him into the room and found a blanket for him to lie upon.

Cantessa dashed up, spoon in hand, and forced the disgusting liquid down his throat.

"Can you heal them?" Carling asked in a whisper, her voice shaking.

"Only time will tell, my dear. Only time will tell."

CHAPTER 35

Building a Wall

CARLING SPENT A SLEEPLESS night moving from one Faun to the next. She didn't see any improvement in their condition but none of them had died so, for the moment, she was content with that. As she worked, she wondered about the mysterious stranger who had given them the poison. Who or what had done this? And why?

Once the sun cast its golden light across the hogback, Shanta came into the chamber that had been converted into a hospital. Her distaste for the Fauns was evident by the wrinkle of her nose and the curling of her lips. She walked stiffly up to Carling. "Are they getting any better?"

"I can't say for sure. I can only hope."

"Yes. We can all only hope," Shanta said, violently rolling her shoulders and pulling at the collar of her cloak. "May I speak with you for a moment, Miss Carling?"

"Of course," said Carling, setting down the damp cloth she had been using to wipe the forehead of a Faun.

The two of them moved toward the council chamber doors. In whispered tones, Shanta addressed her. "The Wizard made it clear that we must begin our preparations immediately. Now that the Fauns cannot help us, how do you propose that we proceed?"

If truth be told, Carling had not even thought about the enormous project that awaited them, consumed as she was with her nursing duties and trying to figure out who had done this dastardly deed. An idea suddenly entered her mind. "We will ask the Centaurs to help us!"

By mid-day a large contingent of Centaurs from the Minsheen herd were gathered in the village square, shovels in hand, sweat cloths tied around their foreheads. They were ready to work.

Word spread throughout the village and the surrounding forest where several cottages, including Higson's, housed still more Duende. All the villagers gathered in the town square to hear what the news might be. Several conversations took place among the little race.

"I haven't seen this much excitement since the great forest fire back in the day," said one old-timer.

"I'm not sure I like it," responded another.

"Ever since that Carling girl saved those Centaur fillies, we haven't had a moment's peace."

"And did you see the condition of those Fauns? Positively ghastly, if you ask me."

"That's the stuff nightmares are made of," said one worried mother as she hugged her child.

Stepping up to a makeshift podium set in front of the government building, Shanta raised her hands in a call for quiet. A hush fell over the crowd. "My dear fellow Duende," she began, "it has come to the council's attention that our village is in grave danger. We have actually become the target of the ire of the warring factions in Crystonia. No longer can we enjoy the peace and quiet and safety of being too small to matter. We are now the focus of attention due to the presence of...well, enough said on that. I will now turn the podium over to Carling, who has come up with a plan to secure our village." Shanta stepped back.

Carling felt her heart start to pound in her chest and her hands get clammy. She pressed her lips together, raised her chin, and stepped forward. "Villagers, I have just returned from a difficult journey during which I witnessed, first-hand, the terrible battles going on just over that hogback." She pointed to the west and all eyes followed her motion. "We have been sheltered from the violence...until now."

"You are the one bringing this to our village!" shouted one man.

"Everything was fine before you got involved with the Centaurs!" yelled another.

The order in the crowd disappeared as several of the villagers voiced their opinions at the top of their little lungs. Carling's breath caught in her chest and she stared out at the crowd that seemed to be getting angrier and angrier by the second. She looked over at Higson and raised her eyebrows, not sure what to do. Higson grimaced and shook his head. *Big help you are*, she wanted to say, but didn't.

Suddenly the crowd became silent.

Carling turned back toward them, wondering what had brought about the abrupt change. She felt a hand on her shoulder. Turning, she looked into the gray cloak of the Wizard. She lifted her eyes and looked up at him, relief flooding over her like warm sunshine.

"What do I do?" she whispered.

"Carry on, child. Carry on."

With newly found confidence born of the presence of the Wizard, Carling continued. "We, with the help of the Minsheen herd, will be building an earthen mound around the entire city...." Carling described in detail the wall that would be constructed. While all eyes remained on the Wizard, all ears listened carefully to what she was saying. As jobs were divided up, Duende left to gather needed equipment and begin their tasks. Eventually, the village square was emptied of everyone but Carling, Higson, Tibbals, and Tandum...and the Wizard.

Carling turned to face Higson. "Higson, I am concerned about your family and the other Duende living outside the village who will not be protected by the wall. We need to go visit each of them and encourage them to move into the protected area once we finish it."

"Good luck with that. I don't see my parents moving an inch. To them, it was their isolation that kept them safe during the last attack."

"But they need to realize it will be different next time," responded Tibbals. "Whichever army comes to the village will destroy anything in its path."

"And we'll have no way to protect them," added Tandum.

"I know that. And you know that. But my parents don't know that," said Higson, scratching his head.

The Wizard settled the discussion. "All you can do is counsel and invite. The decision must be theirs." With a swish of his gray cloak, Vidente disappeared.

"Wow!" said Tibbals. "I wish I could do that!"

Carling smiled and grasped the filly's hand. "Don't we all! Let's go visit those outlying families."

CHAPTER 36

Creating a Fortress

CARLING'S CONCERN OVER WHO had poisoned the Fauns was pushed aside as work began on the wall. Crews divided up tasks with the largest, the Centaurs mostly, doing the heavy work of digging the mound by moving the dirt into a tall, wide pile in the shape of an earthen dam. Once the Fauns were well, they joined the Centaurs in the digging.

The Duende hacked down trees and chiseled sharp points on the ends. With ropes and winches, they stood the logs upright on top of the dirt mound, the sharp tops pointing skyward. At each corner, a watch tower was constructed from additional logs. These were just large enough for a Faun to occupy as it had already been decided this would become their responsibility.

To the west, a massive entry was constructed. The artisans in the village couldn't help but make it pretty, even though Carling kept stressing that it had to be utilitarian and strong. Thick planks of wood were held together with metal bands. But the wood planks had beautiful carvings of trees sculpted into them, and the bands were anything but plain! They curved across the wooden planks like vines on a wall. On either side of the doors, stone watch towers were built in which guards were to be stationed at all times.

None of this was easy, especially for the little Duende. By the end of each day, Duende, Faun and Centaur collapsed from fatigue.

Late in the summer when the air was especially moist and heavy, Carling searched among the Duende laboring on the corner watch towers until she found Shanta. The leader of the council was taking a much-needed break in the shade of the tower.

"Shanta, I need your advice about something," said Carling.

Shanta frowned. "Since when do you need my advice about anything?"

Stung, Carling stepped back, her shoulders slumped. She bit her lower lip to keep it from quivering.

Shanta brushed her hair out of her eyes and looked up at Carling. "I'm sorry. I didn't mean that. I'm hot and tired...we're all hot and tired, I know. I shouldn't take it out on you."

Taking a deep breath, Carling said in a soft voice, "I understand. Don't worry. We're all just trying to do our best to keep the village safe." She sat down in the shade next to the elder. "Shanta," she said, "I have been thinking."

Shanta nodded and waited.

"I would like to build a secret chamber under the government building in which we can hide the children and elderly if we should be attacked. Can you help me find the appropriate place?"

Shanta said nothing for several minutes, her eyes staring straight ahead. Carling waited, letting her think about this new request. Finally, Shanta turned and looked at Carling. "I know just the place."

Shanta struggled to her feet, stretched, and pushed on her back with both hands. "I'm getting too old for this, I'm afraid." She gave Carling a weak smile and started walking toward the government building.

The two of them entered through a side door and walked down a long, narrow hallway. Before reaching the expansive atrium, now emptied of all the injured Fauns, Shanta stopped. To their right was an intricately carved and gilded door. However, unlike all the tall doors that surrounded the atrium, this one was about half the height...just barely tall enough for a Duende to enter. The other unique feature was that it did not have a doorknob. Carling raised her eyebrows in wonder and asked, "What is this?"

"Watch." Shanta pushed on a circular rosette right in the middle of the door. With a low scraping sound, the door slowly swung open. Shanta motioned for Carling to enter.

Once inside, Carling stopped, letting her eyes adjust to the darkness. When her eyes could focus, she saw that she was in a tiny room that was no larger than an oversized closet. The only light was coming from the hallway. "What is this room?" she asked Shanta.

"We started building this many years ago as a place to hide the village treasury. We never finished."

"But how would we fit all the children and elderly in here?" Carling said. "It's so tiny."

"Ah-h-h, but this is not all there is to it. Look down."

On the dimly lit floor, Carling could just make out a series of circles created on the floor from glass tiles. Each circle touched the next at the edges and formed a line leading to one side. The last circle seemed to disappear under the wall. "Press your foot on the last circle," Shanta instructed.

Carling did as she was told. At first nothing happened. Then, very slowly, the wall moved to one side, revealing an opening that was too dark to see into.

Using a piece of flint and steel, Shanta lit a candle that was attached to the wall on one side of the entrance. Immediately, a long staircase became visible. The steps descended downward. Shanta lifted the candle from its holder and the light bounced off the walls. Carling looked over at the elder, who motioned for her to go ahead. Carling led the way down the staircase.

The bottom of the stairs opened into an enormous underground cavern. The walls and ceiling were rough-hewn stone, the floor only slightly smoother. The large room was bare and quite cold. But to Carling, it was flawless.

She walked to the center of the cavern, extended her arms, and twirled around. "It's perfect. Simply perfect," she said. "Let's get some supplies down here...blankets, water, some food and medicines."

By the time the leaves on the trees around the village of Duenton were bright red and gold, the fortress surrounding the village was done. Carling led the villagers in gathering crops and storing food items for the approaching winter.

The Stone of Mercy

By the time the first tiny flakes of snow floated softly to the ground, the fortress walls were straight and strong, the gate secure, and food was in the store houses. Carling looked around, hands on hips, and smiled. Then her smile changed to a frown. She turned to Higson. "Any progress with your family?"

Higson lowered his chin and shook his head. "No. They still refuse to leave their home."

237

CHAPTER 37

The Enemy Returns

CARLING WAS AWAKENED BY the sound of voices from the street below her window. Since the fortress walls had been completed, she had lived in a little room over the town bakery. It was warm and cozy, and every morning she could smell the delicious aroma of baking bread that wafted up to her room from the ovens below. But not this morning, and its absence was ominous.

Carling got out of bed and ran to the little leaded-glass window set in the dormer. She looked out onto the village roofs, which were dusted with a fresh layer of snow that had fallen during the night. The gray clouds were gone now and the pink sky promised a beautiful clear day, but the beauty ended with nature as Carling's eyes moved down to the street.

Below her, villagers were gathering in the town square. Their flailing arms and shouts told Carling that something was terribly wrong. She turned back into the room. The silver breastplate, with the green Stone of

Mercy sparkling brightly, waited on the chair next to her bed. She discarded her night dress and put the breast-plate on over a thick undershirt. The silver metal felt both cold and welcoming at the same time. She put yesterday's tunic on over the breastplate and a warm cloak to top it off. She dashed out the door and down the narrow back stairs that opened into the bakery. As the lack of the customary delicious aroma told her, no bread was baking in the large brick oven. In fact, the baker, named Parkson, and his family were nowhere to be seen. Carling felt her stomach twist and turn. She felt her hands start to sweat and shake. She knew something very bad was happening.

Leaving the bakery through the front door, Carling was assaulted by both the cold winter wind and the shouts of the villagers. "What is it? What's going on?" she asked the first person she approached.

"We're being attacked," responded the villager. His face was red from cold and fear.

Dread filled Carling. She grabbed the villager by both shoulders. "Tell me more. What do you know?"

He turned and pointed toward the west. "See for yourself."

Carling turned and looked in the direction to which he pointed. The early morning sky was scarred by tendrils of twisting black smoke. She let go of the Duende and dashed to the government building, hoping to find the council members there. Before she reached the long steps that led to the entrance, Higson was at her side.

"Carling, they've attacked the outlying homes...my parents...." He let the rest of the sentence dangle in the cold morning air.

Carling stopped and turned to Higson. "Who is it? Who is attacking us?"

"The Heilodius Centaurs."

Carling set her jaw and dashed up the staircase, taking two and three steps at a time. Higson struggled to keep up. "Carling, I've got to go to my parents."

Trying to remain calm as she continued up the steps, Carling responded, "It's too late for them, Higson."

Higson stopped in the middle of the stairs. "What do you mean? Maybe they got away. Maybe they're hiding. Maybe, if we just sent them some help, they'd be okay."

Carling shook her head. "I'm so sorry, Higson. But our job is to protect the village."

"You can't just let my parents get killed!"

"They knew the risks when they chose to stay in their home."

Higson stood for another moment, staring at her with his mouth wide open. Then his eyes narrowed and he said in a low voice. "Well, I'm not going to just stand by and let them be slaughtered by the Heilodius. I'm going to help them." He turned and dashed back down the steps.

"Higson, come back. Don't do this!" At that moment, Carling's heart split in half. Part went with her friend, but the other part pulled her into the government building, where she knew the council would be gathering. The latter won the internal battle; she turned and opened the tall carved doors.

Once inside the chambers, Carling got a full report. One of the Fauns in the northwest watch-tower had reported the first sign of smoke coming from the forest, visible in the early light of dawn. As he watched, several

241

Centaurs, dressed in black, emerged from the woods that bordered the fortress walls. The Centaurs began sending their arrows up and over the walls and into his tower. The Faun scrambled down the tower stairs and signaled the Duende soldiers on duty. Within minutes, the Duende were returning fire from the safety of the fortress. As far as they could tell, no Duende or Fauns were injured but, already, several Centaurs lay dead or dying outside the fortress walls.

As Carling was brought up to date, a Duende rushed into the room. "They are shooting flaming arrows at the fortress!"

The council members began shouting at once, arguing over which course of action to take. Carling stood up, tall and confident. "We do nothing. The fortress walls will be fine. Any flaming arrows that come over the wall will be put out. We must not panic. We must continue returning fire as they expose themselves."

The messenger bowed. "As you say, your majesty." He turned and dashed back out of the room.

For a moment, silence filled the room. Then one council member stepped forward. "Your majesty? He called you 'Your Majesty.' Are we your subjects now?"

Carling turned and looked at the council member. Her eyes were soft and kind. A smile graced her face. "No. We are partners and companions. Together we must keep our village safe. Now, let's get the children and the elderly into the hiding place."

Carling, her skill with the bow and arrow proving to be extraordinary, joined the guards on the city wall. A large Heilodius Centaur galloped straight toward the city gate, a battle-ax in hand. Once he reached the thick plank doors, he began pounding, sending splinters of wood flying in all directions. Carling nocked her arrow, aimed carefully at his ax-wielding arm, and let her arrow fly. With a scream of pain, the centaur dropped the ax, grabbed his arm, and whirled around on his haunches. He galloped away, heading straight for the safety of the forest. Soon, a second centaur approached, intent on finishing the job. Carling sent him running as well.

All morning, great mobs of Heilodius Centaurs galloped around and around the village, shooting arrows up and over the walls. The arrows rained down on the Duende, but nothing stopped the little people in their determination to defend their homes and lives. Shouts rose up on both sides of the wall as instructions were given by leaders. Fortunately, the confusion outside the village wall was not matched by the events inside. Within the village of Duenton, the Duende were orderly and confident, born of their extensive preparation.

By mid-day, the battle ended. The Heilodius Centaurs ceased charging around the village walls, convinced, at last, that they could not penetrate it...at least not with their bows and arrows. They gathered up those of their army who could still gallop and disappeared as suddenly as they had appeared.

A great cheer went up from the Duende as they celebrated their victory.

Carling did not join in the celebration. Instead, she rushed to the city gates. "Has Higson returned? Have you seen Higson?" she asked each of the guards in the stone towers. Each shook their heads, a response that felt as though one of Carling's own arrows had pierced her heart.

"Please open the gates. Let me out."

"Miss Carling," one of the guards protested, "that wouldn't be safe. We can't be sure all the Centaurs are gone."

Carling folded her arms across her chest, raised her jaw and, with determination in her voice, said, "I must find Higson. Open the gates and let me pass."

Reluctantly, the guards opened the gate just enough to let her slip through the gap, out of the safety of the village and into the unknown.

Sorrow and Resolve

THE MINUTE THE DOORS scraped along the cobble-stone and opened the slightest bit, Carling squeezed her slim body through the widening gap. Once outside, she stopped and looked from side to side at the carnage that lay all around her. Dead and dying Heilodius Centaurs littered the ground, lying in their own blood. She yelled up at the guard tower, "Get the healer out here at once. Some of these Centaurs are still alive. We might be able to save them."

With that, Carling turned and worked her way be-tween the bleeding bodies until she reached the forest. She intentionally avoided the narrow road that con-nected Duenton with the various outlying homesteads for fear there might still be Heilodius Centaurs in the area. As she entered the woods, the bodies thinned but the trees thickened. She worked her way toward the for-est glen that she knew held Higson's home. The sun had warmed the winter day only slightly as the battle had ensued. But here, in the forest, an icy chill surrounded her. The cold seemed to grip her and squeeze from all directions. She shivered as she ran, her breaths turning immediately to puffs of condensation that looked like dragon's smoke. Inside, she felt like anything but a dragon. She felt small and weak. She bit her lip to keep from crying. She didn't have time to cry right now.

As she neared the clearing, the crunching sound of her feet on the snow was drowned out by an odd noise weaving through the trees. She stopped for a moment to identify and locate the sound.

Digging. Yes, she was sure of it. Someone was digging and the sound was coming from her right. She changed her direction and dashed off again.

Soon she came upon a wall of scrub oak. Bare of leaves for the winter, the thick, tangled branches still formed a barrier. She peeked over and saw Higson. His back to her, he was unaware of her presence as he dug, sending wet snow and frozen dirt flying behind him. Beside him, lying motionless on the snow, were two bodies. Though they were wrapped in tattered and charred blankets, she knew instinctively who they were.

Carling worked her way back to the clearing to find their home, which was now a smoldering pile of timbers. Images of her own home from several months before filled her mind and a great guttural moan left her throat. But she didn't have time to mourn right now. She pushed the pain back into its special hiding place in her heart and carried on.

She ran behind the house to find the toolshed, which was untouched by the flames that consumed the cottage. The door was ajar and Carling went into the dark, little structure. Between the axes and sickles she found a shovel. With her frozen hands, she grabbed hold of the shovel's wooden handle, pulled the tool from the pile, and dashed back out the door.

She entered the makeshift cemetery without saying a word. Something about the setting and the situation was too sacred to disrupt with speech. A moment later, she stood beside Higson and began digging.

The ground beneath the snow was frozen and the work was much harder than she would have imagined had she thought that far, which she hadn't. She used all her weight, little as it was, to jump on the shovel and peel bits of dirt out of the hole Higson had started. They worked in silence, lost in their own sorrow.

By the time the hole was big enough to hold both of Higson's parents' bodies, the sun was setting and the temperature in the woods was bitterly cold. Carling didn't notice, so concerned was she about Higson. Reverently, Higson set his mother's and father's bodies side by side in the grave.

Just as the last shovelful of dirt dropped with a dull thud on the mound, Higson fell to his knees. He began sobbing, his shoulders shaking violently. Carling stood behind him, not wanting to interfere with his grieving but wishing she could do something to soothe his pain—a pain she knew so well.

As he cried, the tree limbs overhead, heavy with snow, drooped as if in sympathy. One bough dropped its snow at the end of the mound, forming a frozen grave marker. Darkness gathered silently around them.

Once he could control his sobs and catch his breath, Higson turned his muddied and tear-stained face up and glared at Carling. From between clenched teeth he growled, "Why did we have to get involved in this?"

Carling felt like she was going to crumple to the ground and disappear. She wished she could. She reached down and cradled Higson's face in her hands. "I don't know," she said, tears stinging her eyes as she thought of her own parents. "But there is one thing I do know and I know it to the center of my very being. There is no turning back...There is no turning back, now."

To be continued....
The Centaur Chronicles
Book 2
The Stone of Courage

About the Author

Award-winning author, M.J. Evans grew up in Lake Oswego, Oregon. Upon graduation from Oregon State University and marriage to her high school sweetheart, she spent five years teaching teenagers in high school and middle school. She retired from teaching to raise the couple's five wonderful children. Mrs. Evans is an avid equestrian. She loves competing in Dressage and trail riding in the beautiful Colorado mountains where she now lives with her husband, three horses and a standard poodle.

Connect with M.J. Evans on her website:

mjevansbooks.com
or
dancinghorsepress.com

Additional Titles by this Author

The Mist Trilogy:
Mom's Choice Award Gold Medal Winner
Behind the Mist
Mists of Darkness
The Rising Mist

North Mystic
First Place Winner of the Purple Dragonfly Award
Finalist in the Colorado Authors' League Awards

In the Heart of a Mustang
Nautilus Book Awards Silver Medal
Literary Classics Seal of Approval
Finalist in the Colorado Authors' League Awards

Equestrian Trail Guide Books:
Riding Colorado-
Day Trips from Denver with Your Horse
Riding Colorado II-
Day Trips from Denver with Your Horse
Riding Colorado III-
Day AND Overnight Trips with Your Horse

"Like" these books on Facebook:

**Behind the Mist
North Mystic
In the Heart of a Mustang**

Learn about the noble and great horses throughout

history. Follow the author's blog:

www.themisttrilogy.blogspot.com

**The author loves to receive letters from her
readers...and she always writes back! Find
her email address on her website:**

www.dancinghorsepress.com

M.J. Evans